Tiger, Tiger, Burning Bright

A Melanie Kroupa Book

Tiger, Tiger, Burning Bright

A NOVEL

Ron Koertge

Orchard Books

New York

Orchard Books
95 Madison Avenue
New York, NY 10016

Manufactured in the United States of America

10 9 8 7 6 5 4 3 2 1

The text of this book is set in 12 point Monotype Bembo.

Library of Congress Cataloging-in-Publication Data
Koertge, Ronald.
Tiger, tiger, burning bright : a novel / by Ron Koertge.
p. cm.
"A Melanie Kroupa book"—Half t.p.
Summary: Worried that his mother will send his beloved
grandfather to a nursing home "for his own good," Jesse and some
of his eighth-grade classmates accompany Pappy into the mountains
near their small California town to look for the tiger tracks he
claims to have seen.
ISBN 0-531-06840-4—ISBN 0-531-08690-9
(lib. bdg.)
[1. Grandfathers—Fiction. 2. West (U.S.)—Fiction.
3. California—Fiction. 4. Mothers and sons—Fiction.] I. Title.
PZ7.K8187Ti 1994
[Fic]—dc20   93-37758

For Bianca
and, this time, for Sam

Tiger, Tiger, Burning Bright

When I woke up, I could hear my grandfather scuffing around the camp. And I was so glad that I didn't have to go look for him that I just lay there with my eyes closed and listened to him talk to the horses.

Then he started to make coffee. I heard the glug-glug sound of our old canteen, followed by the music of the filter going into the coffeepot and the clack of the blue speckled lid. From half a mile or so away came the soft lowing of some cattle. All of it—the glugs and the tinkles and the clanks and the moos—like a goofy little band tuning up.

When I did take a peek, he was standing with his back to me, looking out over the high desert toward a peak called Igloo Roof because it had a whitish dome and because the idea of an igloo anywhere in this part of central California had tickled somebody's overheated fancy.

1

Pappy looked good outlined against the day: his legs were honest-to-God bowed from seventy-plus years of riding; his Wrangler shirt had been bleached out perfect and made a cool background for his long gray ponytail, pulled back Willie Nelson–style and held by a silver Zuni clip.

"You ready to eat, Jesse?"

"Sure." I grinned. "But how'd you know I was awake?"

"Just a trick," he said. "Stop thinkin' of yourself as separate-like and fall back into the land. Then you're connected to everything."

I stood up and reached for the frying pan. "Yeah, right. I think you just heard me."

He turned around and his big gray mustache flexed as he smiled. "That, too."

I moved the coffee off a little to one side of the crusted grill, put some Crisco in the pan, and laid in the last two little steaks we'd bought at Shop-N-Save.

Pappy rustled through the saddlebags we'd thrown across my horse, Marky Mark. "Where's the beans?" he asked.

"We ate 'em all last night. Or you did."

"Dog*gone*. Why didn't you tell me?"

"I did tell you. We were just about finished when you said you wanted beans. I said that we'd already had beans, but you just went ahead and opened the other can."

He scratched his head. "I forgot I ate my beans?"

"What's the difference? You were gonna eat 'em anyway."

"Difference is I don't have any beans now."

"Well, don't tell Mom, or she'll give you that delayed-gratification speech she's always giving me when we have those little heart-to-hearts about me being almost a man now."

Pappy spat toward the fire. "You know plenty about the birds and bees. I taught you."

"I know, Granddad."

He pointed to Cody and Marky Mark, both dozing in their halters. "Just be like them horses. When your season comes, that's when you want to do it. Otherwise, give yourself a rest."

I turned the steaks one last time as I held an imaginary phone to my ear. " 'Hello, Heather? It sure feels like I'm in season. Want to meet me out by the salt lick?' " I looked up at him. "Real smooth."

He lifted his jeans off his narrow hips, then hunkered down beside me.

"Just eat your steak. You're gonna need every ounce of strength to delay all that gratification of yours."

We didn't say anything while we sawed away at the meat, which was about as thick as a poker chip. And about as tasty.

When we were both done, though, and just sitting back and looking around at nothing in particular,

Pappy said, "What's that behind me on that little scrub oak, a thrush?"

"Uh-huh."

He winked. "Just fall back into the land," he said for the second time that morning. Then he got up slowly. "Nature calls. You start washin' up, okay?"

I scoured the tin plates in the little plastic tub we'd bought in San Luis Obispo a few years ago, gave the horses a few handfuls of oats for the short trip home, and started to break camp.

Pappy and I—and sometimes my buddy, Kyle— had camped out about a thousand times, so I could pack up and look around, too. I sure liked our desert. It wasn't flashy like the one in Arizona with all those picture-postcard saguaros with their arms up in the air like people hanging out laundry, but it was just as interesting in its own way.

The best part was that it was only a few minutes outside of Norbu, so I could get on my horse or even my mountain bike and be out in the middle of nowhere—or at least on the outskirts of nowhere— just about anytime I wanted.

Of course, it wasn't nowhere to me. Thanks to Pappy, I knew maybe fifty square miles of desert better than I knew my own hometown. I knew where the game trails were and which tracks belonged to which animals. I knew the names of the trees and shrubs—which ones you could eat if you

4

absolutely had to and which you could smear on an insect bite or a patch of sunburn. Pappy said that the desert—drought or no drought—was breathing peacefully. All I had to do was breathe right along with it.

I had everything ready to go when Pappy came wandering back and without a word stepped into the saddle, pointed Cody toward home, and—just like that—went to sleep.

I was still impressed by how he could do that: hands balanced on the saddle horn, feet forward in the stirrups, he snored and rocked right along with Cody.

So I just led the way and watched the terrain change. We wound down the gentle switchbacks, and the big sharp rocks—which were young—gave way to smoother, older ones. The long dry grasses of the foothills gossiped together as the horses picked their way through, and pretty soon the trails that the animals made disappeared under the waffly-looking tracks of the ATVs and four-wheel drives.

We skirted a herd of black cattle; then good-sized boulders, big and smooth as elephants, had their places taken by isolated trailers; and finally little shacks sprouted up, or half-framed houses, their wood going gray.

We passed one car chassis, then another—both picked as clean as the little animal skeletons Pappy and I happened on up in the hills. And pretty soon, just beyond a wide green belt of irrigated land, I could see Norbu.

Its main street was called—big surprise—Main Street. Parallel to that were the alphabet streets: A, B, C, all the way to N. And perpendicular to those the numbered ones ran to twenty-one, like a card game.

We'd just ridden under the OSTRICH RACES banner that hung over beautiful G Street when Pappy woke up.

"Biggest cat track back there I've ever seen in my life," he said, just like he hadn't been asleep and we hadn't been riding for forty minutes.

I reined up and let him catch me. "Back where?"

"When I was takin' a leak after breakfast." He held up both hands, making a big circle out of his thumbs and forefingers.

"Wow! Why didn't you show me?"

"Forgot. Just had a big medicine dream to remind me, though. Makes me want to go back up there."

I reached for his reins. "Not now, Pappy. Okay? Mom's expecting us home. We promised."

"You go on. Tell her."

I stopped so fast that Marky turned his head and scowled back at me.

"No! We only got to go camping because we'd be together, remember?"

"Well, Jesse, now I can't let a cat that size roam

around in cattle country. I should at least tell somebody, especially Old Man Yates 'cause we were
camped right next to his place." He took off his hat
and fanned himself. "If I didn't know better, I'd say
that print belonged to a tiger. Why, I've never—"

"A what?"

"A tiger. Or somethin' like that. Sure weren't no
mountain lion."

I reached for his wrist this time. "Pappy, this is
Norbu, California. You've been roaming these hills
all your life. You know there's no tigers around
here."

"Yeah? Well, I know what I saw."

"Promise me you won't tell Mom you saw a tiger.
I mean it. Promise."

"Didn't see no tiger. Saw a great big paw print,
but—"

"Promise me you won't even tell her that."

He licked his mustache thoughtfully. "Better tell
Yates, though."

"Don't tell anybody! 'Cause they'll tell Mom, and
she'll say you're senile."

He patted me on the hand briskly. "Then let's you
and me go back there. Check things out, okay? I
could've made a mistake. It might've been a little
saucer burn from one of them extraterrestrials."

"Don't kid around, Granddad. 'Cause Mom's not
kidding around."

He held up both hands to show how serious he

was. "Tell you what. If you and me can swing around tomorrow or the next day, for now I'll dummy up."

I took off my hat and wiped away a line of perspiration. "Okay, but you gotta promise—"

"Already said I would."

"—and then not forget you promised!"

He held out his hand. "That's a deal."

Pappy and Mom and I lived on the west side of town. We had a squat-looking yellow house on about two and a half acres, which was enough land for a garden (back when it used to rain) and a corral for the horses. Mom had an office and an apartment in the back; she said Virginia Woolf was talking about chiropractors, too, when she wrote that a woman needed a room of her own. My mother: the artist of the vertebrae.

The closer Pappy and I got to the house, the more I hoped Mom had a client or two so she wouldn't start grilling us. And, sure enough, there was Mr. Simpson's old Chevy; so I just watered the horses down and turned them out, then steered Pappy through the front door, the one Mom couldn't see.

"You want anything?" I asked, dropping most of our camping gear onto the floor.

Pappy stretched and patted his pockets, looking

for tobacco. "Nope. Think I'll smoke and watch the TV."

"Good. Take your pills, okay?"

"Sure."

I watched him settle into his chair—the big green one we'd brought in from the old Bouquet Canyon house—and sort of sigh. Just like that, his eyes started to close.

"I'll get 'em for you."

"Get what?"

"Your pills."

"What pills?"

I stopped halfway to the kitchen. "Sometimes I don't know if you're kiddin' me or not."

He winked at me. "Sometimes I don't know myself."

It took me a minute in the kitchen because I put some of the camping stuff away, and by the time I got back into the living room, he was asleep. He'd rolled and lit a cigarette, but it was burning itself out in the giant—and I mean giant—ashtray I'd made for him: a washtub—the old-fashioned kind—half full of sand, which sat right next to his chair.

I went back to my room and took a shower, but I left my cowboy hat on because it was only a few months old and still needed a lot of work. My grand-dad's hat was perfect, and I wanted mine to be perfect, too, which meant so generally trashed that it looked like two or three wild stallions had stomped on it, just missing your brain.

When I got out of the shower, I stood in front of the mirror, rolled the hat up tight, wrung it out like a washcloth, then tried it on. Better, but . . .

So I tried beating it with a rolled-up towel. Then I tried it on again. Better, but . . .

Finally I stood on it while I brushed my teeth. That's when, out of the corner of my eye, I saw Pappy leaning in the doorway.

"I thought you were asleep."

"I heard you hammerin' on something." He looked me over. "Is this some new teen thing, wearin' your hat on your feet?"

I blushed and brushed harder. "Just trying to get it to look right," I mumbled.

"Oh." And he grinned and walked away.

I tried it on one more time—with the towel around me I resembled a Samoan cowboy—and nodded at my reflection. Not bad.

I'd just moseyed—real cowboys always mosey— into my room when the intercom crackled and my mom boomed, "Jesse, are you back?"

I padded across the wonderfully cool floor and punched the button.

"No, Mom, I'm still up in the hills. This is just a terrific intercom."

"The first sarcastic remark of the day is always the best, isn't it?"

I ran one hand across my chest. "Always is for me."

"How's Pappy?"

"Fine."

"No problems?"

"Well, he forgot his pants and then he burned the desert down."

"If that's all, can you come back here a minute? We've got other problems."

"Sure. What's up?"

"You'll see."

While I pulled on a clean T-shirt, jeans, and boots, I watched my wave. Between sessions at some chiropractic seminar in L.A., Mom had picked it up for me at a going-out-of-business gadgets store. It was about as big as an ant farm: narrow like that and see-through. But it was half full of some dense blue liquid, and a little battery-powered engine tilted it left, then right, then left again like one of our local politicians who couldn't make up his mind. I liked to watch the wave build, then crest, then break. It was like a slice of the sea.

In the front room, my granddad was asleep again. On the TV, Dorothy Hamill in a skirt about as big as a Kleenex still zipped around an ice rink, thanks to the magic of videotape.

Like a lot of old cowboys, Pappy wore his hat all the time. It was tilted forward to cover his eyes, so I tilted mine forward, too, but I just about walked into a wall. That was obviously a lying-down style.

I sidestepped the lariat that lay coiled on the old carpet and then made one more detour, this time around a pair of Pappy's boots that stood like sentinels beside the kitchen door.

Outside, it was barely nine o'clock, but already hot. The sun was a hole in the sky that somehow focused the heat, intensified it like a magnifying glass.

I waved at Mr. Simpson, who'd just fired up his old Chevy half-ton. Since I'd seen him, he'd gotten a red door at the junkyard and what looked like a Ford bumper, so the truck was patched together, like the clothes I saw around town and in school. Poor old Norbu was so hot and so dry, the land was so tired, and the economy was so depressed that not many people could afford new things.

There was nobody waiting in Mom's office, so I straightened up a stack of magazines like *Vegetarian Times*, which anybody else in Norbu would probably use to wrap beef in. Then I walked down the little hall between her two treatment rooms. Inside both of them hung the same long picture of a spine.

My mother heard me and, even before I knocked, said, "Welcome, weary traveler." Inside, her apartment was, as usual, spotless and cool. The couch was green with a big rain forest print. The lamps looked like bamboo. A picture of a waterfall hung over the stereo.

Mom was still wearing her long white doctor's coat. She gave me the once-over. "The new wet-hat look," she said. "I read about it in *Vogue*. Or was it *Field & Stream*?"

"What's up?" I asked, massaging the damp brim with both hands.

"Follow me."

We filed back into her kitchen. On the gray Formica table lay a cheese about as big as a Honda tire. I was relieved that, for a change, this visit didn't seem to have anything to do with Pappy.

I pointed to the fingerprints all over the cheese. "If this was the murder weapon, we can close the case by noon."

Mom grinned. "Mr. Simpson got it a couple of days ago when somebody borrowed his tractor."

"A cheese with a past."

"What do we do with it?" she asked, circling the table. "There's enough cholesterol in here to wipe out Communism."

"Communism's already dead, Mom."

"And you know why, don't you? They got a cheese from Mr. Simpson."

Just then there was a quack, so I took a bowl off the wooden dish rack, filled it with water, and passed it to my mother.

She opened the back door, patted a gander we'd named Mrs. Johnson's Coccyx, then let him drink. He, like the cheese, had been payment-in-full for an adjustment and some acupressure. There was a lot of bartering in Norbu, and Mom didn't have the heart to say no.

I looked back at the cheese, which seemed to be sagging. "We could freeze it, I guess."

"And then we'd have a frozen cheese."

"True."

Mom, who went in for precarious hairdos, touched one blond wave. "Want to give it away?" she asked.

"On Sunday? Sure."

Every weekend at the old Starlight Drive-In there was this swap meet where people could get things for nothing. Kyle and I went sometimes with his mom and my mom. We manned the free-food table. It was pretty depressing. No grown-ups ever came over; they sent the kids. Then the parents stood way off to one side and waited. The men—the husbands—just stared down at the ground while the women peered over to see what they were getting and figured how many meals they could wring out of it.

Mom patted the cheese. "What do we do with this guy till then?"

I held my nose. "Maybe a little chat about personal hygiene?"

"Is there room in the fridge in the front house? This one's packed."

I grabbed it and heaved.

"Lift with your knees!"

"Don't worry. I don't want you adjusting *my* spine."

Mom gave me one of those thank-you pats on the shoulder. Then as she opened her refrigerator she said, "Guess what Simpson told me. Heather Hughes likes you."

"Really? That's great!"

She looked suspicious. "You believe this? Why would Mr. Simpson, of all people, know?"

"That's how it works in eighth grade, Mom. People tell each other who likes who. Nobody ever goes right to the person they like."

"Mr. Simpson isn't in eighth grade."

"But he lives next door to Mary Rocamora, and she's Heather's best friend."

"So Mary tells Mr. Simpson when they're—what? Doing their nails together? Shopping at Clothes Time?"

"Very funny."

Mom smiled and took a swipe at my hat. "Sorry. I'm glad to see you thinking about girls and dating."

"I'm not exactly thinking about dating," I said firmly. "I just like knowing that Heather likes me."

"Well, you *should* be thinking about it. You're thirteen. Next year's a hot year."

"You don't date," I pointed out.

"But I *did* date. I *have* dated. I'll date again."

"Don't stop now; try for future perfect."

She opened a peach nonfat yogurt. "And your granddad had the world's longest date—married fifty-one years to Grandma. So it's your turn around here. You're about to become the designated dater."

"Okay, then, you know what I like about Heather? She smells like Windex."

Since my hands were full, she leaned in and kissed me on the cheek. "I knew love was blind, but I didn't know its nose had fallen off, too."

"God, I'm sorry I told you that. *It's not love.* I'm just glad—"

"All right. All right. Let me get the door for you."

I was halfway to the house when I smelled smoke. I groaned, "Not again," tucked the cheese under one arm like a football, and sprinted for the kitchen.

Tossing the cheese onto the counter, I turned off the burner under my granddad's pan of beans and opened the two north windows before I glanced into the living room. He was asleep in his chair, both arms and legs so sprawled that he looked like he'd been tossed there.

I started huffing and puffing and waving a newspaper—anything to get the smoke out of the kitchen so that Mom wouldn't know he'd burned his breakfast again.

I'd just scrubbed out the old, battered aluminum pan and was flapping around like Big Bird, trying to get the last of the smoke out the door, when Mom asked, "What are you doing?"

I jumped. "God! You scared me. I didn't hear you come in."

She pushed back her long white doctor's coat and put both hands in the pockets of her jeans. "I repeat, what are you doing?"

"Uh, dancing?"

"I asked you first."

"Dancing. Practicing for Kyle's mom's birthday party. Heather's gonna be there." I rubbed my right shoulder. "Dancing's hard. I want to get in shape."

"I thought you were trying to take off."

"Yeah? Well, as a matter of fact, it's a new dance called, uh, The Airplane."

"Oh, sure."

If I could just keep her talking. "You're a chiropractor. What do you know about new dances?"

She glanced at the cheese where it had skidded into the canisters. "What happened here?"

"I don't know," I said innocently.

"You're telling me that you didn't do this? That the cheese attacked the coffee can on its own?"

"Maybe it's an evil cheese. Maybe Mr. Simpson got it from Stephen King."

Mom laughed, which was good; but almost immediately she stopped, raised her head, and sniffed like a wary doe. "I smell smoke. What burned? Did Pappy—"

"Toast," I lied. "I was washing up and I forgot. . . ."

"My God, not you, too?"

Just then Pappy ambled into the kitchen, rubbing his face with both hands like he'd been swimming. "Where's my beans?"

I shot to the cabinet and grabbed a can. "Haven't fixed 'em yet. I'll do it right now."

I ground the top off with our ancient can opener and dumped the gooey beans into Granddad's favorite pan.

"You should eat beans every day, Jesse."

I nodded my head. "I know, Pappy."

He put his hat back on. "Just look at me. I've had beans pretty near every day of my life and . . ." Pappy narrowed his eyes suddenly, then blinked.

As he looked around, frowning, Mom glanced at me with one of those I-told-you-so expressions. But I had a few expressions of my own squirreled away, and I dug out Give-him-a-minute.

Pappy tugged at his mustache and asked me, "What was I sayin', Jess?"

"That you'd eaten a lot of beans."

More frowning and tugging. "You're gonna have to jump-start me here, son. I've eaten a lot of beans and . . . ?"

"And look at you."

18

He brightened. "That's right, yeah. And look at me." He thumped himself on the chest.

"When are you gonna get rid of that pan, Dad? Aluminum's not good for you. I'll buy you some Corning Ware."

Pappy used one finger like a spoon. "Don't want Corning Ware, honey. That pan's got character, like me."

Mom got a little red in the face. "What if that article I showed you is right, and there's a direct correlation between aluminum and Alzheimer's?"

He opened his hands wide in that way everybody does to show how innocent they are. "I've used this here pan for more than thirty years, and there's nothin' wrong with me."

As Mom sagged in frustration, Pappy headed for the door. He grabbed me by the back of the neck, roughly and affectionately. "Where's my hat?" he asked.

"Aren't you standin' on it?" I asked. "I always stand on mine."

Pappy smiled and looked down at his white socks. "Wouldn't hurt it if I did. Now, where'd I put my boots?"

I said that I'd get them, and I just reached around the corner for his old Justins. Then I stood there while he leaned on me and slipped into them.

"I'm gonna give those horses a bath," he said over his shoulder. "Not good to put 'em up hot."

"See!" I crowed. "I forgot that, but he remembered."

Mom frowned until the crunch of his footsteps on the gravel driveway had died out. Then she turned back into the kitchen, where a vague haze made the branding irons on the wallpaper look fuzzy around the edges.

She leaned on the counter hands flat on the green tiles that Pappy and I had put in. "What am I gonna do with him?" she muttered.

I stepped up beside her. "Mom, nothin' happened. Just some burned toast."

She turned her head to look at me. "Honey, you didn't burn toast two weeks ago. You didn't burn toast on New Year's Day. I can't just sit by while he incinerates himself and you, too."

"You're more liable to get killed by falling space debris than you are to get burned up by a grandfather. I read that in the paper."

"Very funny, ha-ha." She reached for her hair, then thought better of it. "He leaves the freezer open."

"Better than leaving his fly open."

"He does that, too, but then forty pounds of frozen chicken doesn't go bad."

I patted her on the shoulder, glancing at the clock while I did. "I gotta go, okay?"

Mom came and sat at the table. "And he messes with my answering machine."

"Obviously it's not okay." I sank into the nearest chair.

"I came home the other day," she said, "and the whole tape was full of him and some other old guy talking about cows. A patient couldn't have called in if he'd wanted to."

"Well . . ."

She pointed toward the door. "*My* tape. He's been back in *my* apartment. Fooling around with *my* machine."

I took her hand. "Pappy doesn't think about things like your apartment or his room or my room."

She wagged a finger at me, like a windshield wiper. "Because he forgets where he is. He gets lost in his own house."

"Mom, he's just old. And, anyway, he bought this place. All of it."

She started to act all flouncy and put-out. "Thank you for reminding me of how much I owe Pappy, but I'll tell you this: one more panful of burned beans and we're even!" She punctuated the last two words with sharp raps on the table. "And anyhow, there's all kinds of obligations. Bottom line, I'm obliged to do what's best for him, and that's not always what he wants or what you think he wants."

I sat back and crossed my arms. "You're not gonna put him in that prison for old geezers."

"Golden Oaks is not a prison. It's a retirement facility."

"Man, I just hate it when you talk about putting him away."

"Jesse, you don't understand."

"*I* don't? *You're* the one who doesn't understand. He's your father, and you're treatin' him like a piece of furniture or a Christmas ornament or something: 'Oh, let's put Pappy away now. Pappy's out of style. The Pappy season is over.' God, Mom. Have you got a heart in there, or some little Amana ice maker?"

That got her out of the chair and right in my face. "And here's what *you* don't understand: my father is an accident waitin' to happen. So I want him safe. That's why Golden Oaks is better for everybody."

"Mom, he's a cowboy. Always has been, always will be."

"Oh, yeah? How many cowboys tie their horses to the Arco pump and then leave 'em there?"

"Oh, yeah? Well, how come you can forget about a patient and then come back without the milk you said you went to get, but that's okay?"

"Once. That happened once."

"And what are you gonna do when I forget my homework some morning—put me away, too?"

"That's completely different, Jesse, and you know it."

"It isn't either." I snatched my hat off. The heat of the argument had just about dried it, so it looked too good to mash up in frustration. I took a deep breath instead. "I'm just saying you don't understand, that's all."

Mom sighed. "And I'm saying *you* don't understand."

We stood around like that for half a minute or so, both of us looking down at our feet like bad dancers. Finally I muttered, "Are you goin' down to the ostrich races?"

She shook her head and muttered right back, just longer. "I wouldn't go ten feet to see Bobby Yates walk on water. I get him fixed up so he can drive his truck without sciatica makin' him get out and lie on the side of the road every ten miles, and what does he do? He stiffs me for four hundred and sixty-five dollars, that's what he does."

I tried a smile, a little one. "Don't you think this is about a once-in-a-lifetime opportunity, though? I mean, ostrich races in Norbu?"

"Honey, Bobby's a snake-oil salesman. This is just snake oil with feathers."

I nodded. "Then I gotta meet these guys from school. For finals, Mr. Wright divided the class up into study groups. Kyle and I got lucky and drew each other, but otherwise we got some real winners."

"Just be home for dinner, okay?" Then she poked me in the chest. "Don't slump. You remind me of a drummer I used to go out with."

I backed away. "Just keep your hands off my ver- tebrae, okay? Man, I'm lucky you're not a surgeon."

"You just look a little out of alignment."

I retreated a little more. "If Pappy wants to go to the races, will you take him?"

"He'll forget."

"But if he doesn't."

"All right. All right." Then she grabbed me. I thought she was going to kiss me, so I turned my head away real quick; but instead she squeezed hard and my back cracked in two or three places. "That's better," she said, dusting off her hands like she'd been chopping wood.

A few minutes later, I spotted Kyle waiting for me under what passed for a tree in Norbu. I glided up and made the knobby tire of my mountain bike bump into his.

"What's happening, mon?" Kyle was in a Jamaican mood, so he made the question sing a little.

"The usual. Camped out with Pappy up in the Santa Rios. He saw a tiger and then burned some more beans."

"A tiger! Seems like a good reason to burn beans to me. I sure would've."

"Want to go back up there tomorrow? He's not gonna be satisfied until he checks things out again."

"You mean he really thinks he saw a tiger?"

I shook my head. "Some old puma tracks, maybe. I just don't want him sayin' the *T* word around Mom."

" 'Cause the road to Golden Oaks is paved with imaginary tigers?"

"For sure."

"Was she still upset about my mom havin' to drive him home the other day?" Kyle asked.

I polished part of my handlebar with the heel of my right hand.

"Probably, but gettin' lost doesn't really hurt anybody. Mom's afraid he's gonna burn the house down with me in it."

"Aw, Pappy'd never do anything to hurt you."

"Or Mom, either. But she keeps sayin' how Golden Oaks is really for Pappy's own good." I shook my head. "That's what she said when she made me eat leek soup that time I had the flu."

"Think grown-ups would be weird, anyhow, or is it living in Norbu that did it?"

We turned to look at the town where both of us had spent our entire lives. The sun had lapped away at the white houses and sanded the red and blue garages and sheds. Because nobody wanted to waste water washing their cars and trucks, fleets of beige machines crept through the baking streets.

We'd always been a little too far south to get the rain that sometimes swept down from San Francisco, and a little too far north to take advantage of tropical storms that half drowned Los Angeles once or twice a year. And for the last five years it had been worse. People had let their lawns go completely, and almost nobody grew flowers anymore.

A few folks had covered their dead Bermuda grass with gravel, then painted that a weird bright green, the color of play money. Kyle spotted one of the retired high school teachers puttering around with a spray can.

I made my voice deep, like a parent. "Spray that lawn, young man! Why, when I was your age, we had to paint our lawn with a brush!"

Kyle grinned a little and glanced at his Timex, bright silver against his dark skin. "Post time for Norbu's first and last ostrich race is in half an hour."

"Mom says Bobby's gonna try and sell stuff first."

"Probably ostrich spit: grows hair and kills those pesky weeds, too."

I waved away a fly that was dive-bombing me. Without even turning my head, I could see the roof of the high school. "I sure wish Mr. Wright wasn't leaving."

Kyle kicked at the ground with the toe of one black Reebok. "What else is he gonna do? They cut all the teachers' pay from not much to a lot less." Then he pointed to his watch. "Let's head out and get a good spot. I'm about to melt sittin' still."

We rode single file for a couple hundred yards. Then we waited at a stop sign with three or four bullet holes in it while a massive Norbu traffic jam— two pickups and a beat-up Datsun—sorted itself out. The last truck through had three guys crammed in the front and three more sprawled in the back. They were all seniors and they all gave us the finger.

"Pitiful," said Kyle.

We cruised down the main street—past the feed store, Jerry's Toggery, Western Auto, Toon's Grill. There were a lot of trucks and a few horses nosed up to the Long Branch Saloon.

Nearly every third or fourth store was boarded up. But some little kids, first and second graders, had taken butcher paper and painted pictures of themselves doing a rain dance. And that made the dusty windows look a little better.

We waited at the four-way stoplight right in the center of town, catty-corner from the Arco station and right beside the bank, whose shadow seemed somehow heavier and cooler than a regular building's.

I peeked between the big slabs of plywood that covered the doors. "You just don't think about a bank going out of business."

"Wish they'd had a yard sale." Kyle stood up on his pedals, balancing without letting his feet touch the ground, and a dozen people surged past.

There was usually nothing to do in Norbu and

plenty of time to do it in, so you couldn't blame folks for pouring in for any kind of free show.

Kyle and I slipped like minnows among the pickups and cars. Most of the stores that'd survived had big hand-lettered signs in their windows like DON'T STICK YOUR HEAD IN THE SAND! LOOK AT THESE BARGAINS!!

The crow.d was two or three deep along most of the street, but we found a place in front of Dean's Sundries and parked our bikes.

"Wanna get some gum or something?" I asked.

Kyle put his hand to his heart. "I don't know if I can stand the rush."

I shoved him toward the little hole-in-the-wall store. The shelves were littered with boxes—mostly empty—of stuff like Black Jack and Chiclets. There were pocket combs, nail clippers, dusty-looking cigars, key chains with mermaids on them, and Camel straights under a hand-lettered sign that said SMOKES—25 CENTS A PEACE. Dean sat behind the counter. He was grubby and needed a shave. He glanced at us, and stopped arranging dimes and nickels into little piles.

"No way," he said, "not till you're seniors. And maybe not then, 'cause if he found out, Pappy'd kill me, and then Kyle's dad'd come along and kill me again."

Kyle and I looked at each other. "We just, uh, wanted some gum."

28

Dean half closed one eye and cocked his head. "No weed?"

"Jeez, no."

"Well, you can't have it."

"But we don't want it."

"Then get your gum and go!"

I picked some Juicy Fruit, wiped the dust off on my shorts, then laid a quarter on the mat with its printed THANK YOU almost worn away.

"So," Kyle murmured as we left, "have I got this straight? If we wanted dope, he wouldn't sell it to us; but since we don't want it, he's mad."

I nudged him. "Check it out."

Standing in the alley were three ostriches in a converted horse trailer. Another one, the biggest, was tied up all by himself a few yards away.

"Man," I said, "are those guys ugly."

"I don't know. They look like your typical post-nuclear monster chickens to me."

The big guy hissed and kicked, shook himself so his little saddle slipped, and struck like a cobra when anybody got too close.

"And we're supposed to eat these dudes?" Kyle asked.

"That's what it said in the paper."

"Bobby must be nuts. This is cattle country. Nobody's gonna raise those things."

About ten yards away, standing with three littler kids, was Walter Brown, one of the guys that Mr.

Wright had stuck us with for our study group. He was decked out in a shiny red shirt and a little red hat. When he turned around, there was a big number four pinned to his back.

Kyle spotted him, too. "Oh, man. An ostrich jockey. Now there's an asset to any academic endeavor."

Just then Walter saw us and said something to the three other riders in their black, yellow, and green shirts. Then he galloped our way, slapping himself on the thigh with a switch.

"Hi, guys!" he boomed. "Hi. How are you? You okay? Is this great or what? Listen, pick me up at my house after, okay? We'll ride to the cave together." He was all over the place, really hyper; but his eyes had dark circles under them.

"Walter, why do we have to meet at the cave? It's about a hundred and ten out. We could go to Kyle's, where it's air-conditioned."

He shook his head so hard his hat flew off. "No, no. If we go to a house, grown-ups can hear us."

"So what? We're not making bombs. We're a study group."

"But I already told the other guys we'd meet at the cave. Just get me after, okay? You know where I live. So I'll see you there. Oh, but don't bug my dad if he's outside working, okay? He fought last night at the Long Branch. I'll keep an eye out for you. And I'm glad I'm in you guys' study group:

we're the best, there ain't no rest. Right? Oh, yeah, Jesse—where's Pappy? I want him to see me ride."

"He's—"

"Oh, wait. I gotta go, okay? Bet your allowance on me. I got the big bird; he's fast. I can tell. It's money in the bank. Okay? Okay? See you later."

Then he was gone, slapping himself on the leg, making a beeline for the other so-called jockeys, who were standing around Bobby Yates, squinting up at his red sport coat like it was the sun.

"I'll bet that kid lives on Twinkies," Kyle said.

Just then Bobby walked out into the center of Main Street, raised his arms for quiet, then jogged back and jumped up onto the bed on his big red Ford pickup. One of his hired men handed up a microphone plugged into a guitar amp.

"Now, folks," he began, but the sound system made those yodelly *Close Encounters* sounds, and everybody laughed.

"Now, folks, before I call the races here, I want to say a few words—"

"I hope!" shouted one of the regulars from the steps of the Long Branch Saloon.

"—a *very* few words about economic opportunities in these trying times."

A baby started to wail, so Bobby just about stuck the microphone in his mouth. "All of you know what we're up against here," he bellowed. "Between the drought, the downturn in our economy, and the special-interest groups in Sacramento, our way of life, one built on farming and ranching, is rapidly disappearing."

The light reflected off Bobby's Ray•Bans as he pointed to the starting line, where three of the four ostriches milled around.

"Now, I have here a viable alternative. You can use everything about them but their squawk." He balanced on one foot and showed us his boot. "Their hide makes beautiful footware, their feathers are worth their weight in gold, and they're good eatin', too. Why, ostrich tastes—"

Half a dozen other guys shouted it out right along with him: "Just like chicken!"

Bobby, turning red, looked down. Then he rallied and held up a brochure as some of the men who worked for him opened up a big box. "Don't decide today. Just take one of these free handouts and talk it over with your loved ones after dinner. Most of you've got land lying idle, land you think has been burned up. Well, picture a cash crop of these noble animals against the horizon, just gettin' fat on whatever's there 'cause—just remember, friends—they're used to grazing on sand and doing just fine."

Kyle tugged at my shirt so I'd see Nigel—another one of the guys in our group—and his dad, who was dressed all in khaki like a big-game hunter. He was taking pictures a mile a minute with one of those fancy cameras where you don't have to wind the film forward yourself. Behind him, toting a wide leather satchel, was Nigel—in linen shorts with a crease, no less. While his dad closed in on old Mrs. Meyers, who really did have one of those faces with what my mom called character, Nigel angled toward us. His blond hair led the way. He had a big wave in the front that never seemed moussed or gelled—it just hung there, ready to break on the shore of his forehead.

"Why do we have to meet at that cave?" he demanded.

"No small talk, Nigel, okay? Just get to the point."

"It was Walter's idea," I said.

He shifted the leather camera case and rubbed one shoulder. "Well, why is Walter in charge?"

Kyle pointed across the street and said emphatically, " 'Cause whoever can talk the fastest wins."

We all looked at Walter, who was helping work the crowd. Lots of people sheepishly held up one hand, then snatched the shiny little pamphlets and stuffed them away like they were dirty pictures or something.

"Nigel! Bring me that other Nikon!"

Nigel glanced at his dad. "Oh, well," he said, "so we go to the cave." Then he hurried toward his father, who was waiting with one hand out.

"What a weird life," I said. "How many schools did Mr. Wright say Nigel had gone to—like ten?"

Kyle nodded. "That'd be cool in a way."

I shook my head. "I like Norbu."

"Uh-uh. You like all the stuff Pappy taught you about this place."

"No, I really—"

But Bobby interrupted me. "Thanks for your patience, folks. Those of you who are interested in a bright future, you just give me a call. Right now, though, let's get on with the races!"

He paused for some hoots and scattered applause as Walter came dancing out, waving and bowing like a total show-off, along with the other three jockeys, who were pretty much stuck together like paint samples. Bobby's hired hands struggled to line the birds up and get the saddles straight.

I looked around for Granddad or Mom as Bobby's arms shot up, making his red sport coat leap like a flame. He shouted, "Let the games begin!"

It wasn't that easy. Three of the birds just milled around flapping their stunted wings, their eyes bulging.

Nothing stopped Bobby. "Our first runner," he shouted. "One of two distaff competitors today. Mother of champions. The swiftest of the swift. Put your hands together for Venus!"

" 'Put your hands together'? " I quoted. "What's he been doin', watching MTV?"

"Number two is Solomon!"

"Not a fast ostrich," Kyle said, "but a wise one."

"Three we call Diamond Lil, and number four is Big Bad John."

Number four was Walter's mount, and though he'd been the one tethered off by himself earlier, the one who'd kicked and hissed, now he just stood there on his big splayed feet and glared at Bobby.

"Are we ready?" Bobby yelled, revolving slowly to include everybody. "All bets down. Get 'em even now, boys. Let's have a fair start."

"Never happen," muttered Kyle, and he was right. When three of the kids were mounted, the fourth was holding on to one of those sinewy-looking necks for dear life. When they were all four in their saddles, two of the birds would be facing the wrong way.

Bobby was holding a handkerchief up as high as he could. I guess he planned to drop the handkerchief and the big birds would streak past him, but maybe his arm got tired because finally he just screamed, "They're off!"

Solomon immediately dumped his rider and ran, appropriately enough, toward the library. Diamond Lil fell down, Venus stood there quivering and looking kind of green around the bill, while Big Bad John, little black wings spread like the summer cloak of the Grim Reaper, headed straight for Bobby, who took off down the middle of the street, yelping and slapping at the huge beak that was trying to take a piece of his backside.

The two old guys in front of us took it all—the hooting crowd, the screaming kids, the drunks who were doubled over laughing—in stride.

One said, "Haven't seen Bobby run like that since his senior year."

"If he'd a run that good then," said the other, "the football team wouldn't have gone oh-for-twelve."

A little later, Kyle and I pulled up in front of Walter's just about even and then brought the back wheels of our bikes around in skids that raised two rooster tails of dust. We hadn't planned that, so it made us both grin.

The run-down house didn't look as bad as the Bates place in *Psycho*, but it wasn't going to win any prizes. It needed paint and it sagged on one side, like a mail carrier. In one of the narrow front windows hung a plastic Christmas wreath with two bogus red candles.

"Festive," I said.

"Why didn't Mr. Wright match us up with three of the girls instead of three other guys?"

"He probably thinks this is character building."

Kyle glanced over at me and grinned. "Oh, guess what? Heather likes you."

"God, where'd *you* hear?"

"Dad told me. Said he heard it at the feed store."

"Mr. Simpson told my mom."

"Just think. One of these days you and Heather are going to actually talk."

I shook my head. "Too much to hope for. Maybe we'll just dance at your mom's party and afterward we'll hear if we had a good time or not."

I started toward the door, but Kyle grabbed my handlebars. "This way."

We worked our way around back quietly, weaving through the tubs of dead geraniums and the white-washed tires until we spotted Walter's dad, leaning over a motorcycle. There were parts all around him in an egg-shaped fallout pattern—nuts, bolts, a piston, tires, a chassis, gearboxes.

I cleared my throat a couple of times, then said, "We're, uh, looking for Walter."

He didn't turn around. "Walter's inside."

We watched his muscles flex under a faded T-shirt with an American flag above the words THESE COLORS DON'T RUN. He wore greasy jeans, and one of his cowboy boots, which had split or just worn out, was wrapped with silver duct tape. On his left biceps was a tattoo of a snake that writhed as he worked.

"Did you, uh, see the ostrich races?" I asked politely.

He answered without raising his head. "I don't want a whole lot to do with Bobby Yates. Is your granddad home now or still uptown?"

"Home probably."

"I need to call him. He said he might know of some work."

Kyle glanced over at me as Walter's mother pushed open the screen door and struggled down the three cement blocks that took the place of regular stairs. She had a broom in one hand, a mop in the other, and buckets filled with cleaning stuff.

Kyle and I propped our bikes up and headed her way. "You need a hand?"

She waved us away. Walter's mother was big, but her clothes were small. Her black pants were open at the waist and her Grateful Dead T-shirt was totally stressed. As the door slammed behind her, she reached around with one hand and massaged her back.

"What do you think your mom'd charge to fix me up?" she demanded.

Two ducks and a cheese, I thought, but I said, "Don't worry about that. Just call her."

She collected her things painfully. "Do you think she'd trade? I houseclean."

"Sure. I mean, sure she might. Call her. Really. Say you just talked to me."

With a nod, she limped past her husband, gave him a kiss on the cheek, and put herself, piece by painful piece, into the front seat of a rusted-out Plymouth Fury.

She'd just pulled away when Walter shot out the back door like somebody going for Olympic gold in the long jump. He landed hard, pitched forward, then grinned,

"I won the race! Did you see me?"

"Uh-huh."

Walter adjusted his long green see-through visor, the kind those poker-playing dogs are always wearing. "And did you see Big Bad John let me lead him back to the trailer after Bobby ducked into the Western Auto store? I got a real way with animals." He touched his dishwater-blond hair. "Like telepathy. John said he was lonely for Africa."

"Sure." Kyle grinned. "But did he say why he wanted to bite Bobby in the butt?"

"Don't forget to pay that phone bill, Walter, all right?" His father turned around and shook a Phillips screwdriver for emphasis.

I saw his face for the first time: a split lip, one partly closed eye, a bruise high on his cheekbone.

Walter patted his back pocket. "Don't worry."

Walter was wearing formerly good pants cut off at the knee to make shorts. Maybe *formerly* should be replaced by *Precambrian*. And maybe *cut off* should be *chewed off*. Anyway, he brushed at them as he muttered, "I put in the ten dollars I got for bein' a jockey. That'll help."

Then he motioned to Kyle and me and we backed

our bikes toward the street. "So I'm going now, okay, Dad?" Walter yelled. "I cleaned up and everything, okay?"

Walter's dad leaned farther into his Harley. "Just pay that phone bill sometime today and get back here sometime this year."

When we got to the street, Walter coughed a couple of times. "His head hurts is all," he explained.

"So he lost last night?"

"No. Won a hundred bucks. That's why we can get the phone turned back on." Suddenly he did a stationary wheelie and croaked, "You know what I was just thinking? That if a football team had uniforms that were green with white stripes on them, then the guy with the ball could just like lie down and disappear. Cool, huh?"

Kyle laughed and gave him a playful shove toward the park. "You just keep thinkin', Walter."

We rode for a few blocks with Walter in the lead, but we learned pretty fast that there was no point in following him. He couldn't help jumping curbs, doing figure eights, and popping wheelies. Then he'd shoot a block or so ahead, slam on his brakes, and wait for us, looking anxious.

Walter led us past the Baptist church. Some white letters had tumbled off the black background of the glassed-in bulletin board, so it said RAY FO RAIN. Then we angled through the park, where one or two tired-looking dads smoked and halfheartedly helped their kids onto the swings.

Suddenly—like there was any other word for anything he did—Walter shot up and over the curb, pedaled like crazy toward the drained swimming pool, leaped off his bike, and threw himself onto the tall fence.

We watched him scramble all the way to the top and get a grip on the barbed wire.

"Over here!" he shouted. "Look at this!"

"This is a nightmare," said Kyle as we glided that way. "We could be camping with Pappy or reading a book or both. Instead we've got Mr. Pee Wee Wild Kingdom here."

"Speaking of camping with Pappy—" I said, but Walter interrupted me.

"Look!" His skinny arm was extended so far it quivered. He was as excited as Columbus first sighting land. "Look there!"

All I could see were a few coins still lying on the flaky blue bottom near the ten-foot marker. Were those the same ones Kyle and I had dived for two years ago?

I told Walter it was just money. "Forty-five whole cents."

"No! Out in the middle. A nose clip. See it? I could use a nose clip!"

"What do you want a nose clip for?" Kyle said.

"There isn't any water. And anyway, only fat kids wear nose clips."

"He's right, Walter, and that's one of life's great mysteries."

"Walter!"

An amplified voice—crackly like the intercom at home but fifty times louder—made us all whirl around.

"Get down off that fence!"

It was Sheriff Junker with his megaphone. As he ambled toward us, leaving his black-and-white Nova idling behind him, Walter dropped onto the sidewalk and scrambled for his bike.

Kyle and I glided toward the sheriff, who said, "If he falls off there and breaks his head, the town hasn't got a lot of extra money to buy him a new one."

"If he falls on his head, he'll be okay," Kyle said.

The sheriff grinned, showing the most amazing set of teeth: one real, one gold, one real, one gold—like the pattern on a patio floor. Seeing it always made me want to rush home and floss.

"We'll keep an eye on him," I said.

"I'd appreciate it."

Just then, with all four ostriches peering out of the trailer, Bobby Yates drove up, braked hard, and got out of his truck, leaving the red door standing open.

"Claude!" he shouted. "Get in that squad car, turn on the red lights, and lead me to Osco. I got a buyer for these damned birds and I don't want to waste a minute gettin' them up there.''

The sheriff took a deep breath, resettled his hat, then turned away from us and headed for the squad car. Meanwhile, Bobby was lecturing his cargo: "You're gonna be ugly boots that won't walk anywhere, ugly feathers that won't dust nothin', and I'm gonna be glad, you hear me? All I needed was one more humiliating experience for my stock to go to nothin' in Norbu, and I got it thanks to you miserable stinkin' excuses for feathered friends!''

Then he climbed back into the truck and followed Sheriff Junker.

Walter cocked his head and nearly closed his eyes. "Big Bad John says not to worry; he'll be back.''

"This is you communicating with the ostrich, right?" asked Kyle.

"Right.''

"The same you who told the whole cafeteria he saw Elvis down at the A&W, and it turned out to be Ronnie Saunders's mother.''

"Well, it was dark, and the way she was holding her hot dog made it look like a microphone.''

"I rest my case.''

As we followed Walter toward the cave, Kyle looked over at me and said, "This is where we boiled Barbie.''

"But only in the interest of science, remember? We timed it. She was tough.''

"And then you blew up Ken with a cherry bomb. It was great."

I nodded. "I'd like to blow him up again. He still gets on my nerves."

We skirted four huge eucalyptus trees that still flourished, probably thanks to some leaks in the water pipes that ran underground toward the pool and the fountains.

Down past those and across a used-to-be creek was the cave. It went back eight feet or so into the side of the cliff. Outside, somebody had once sunk four posts, and every so often some kids would try to make a roof out of dry palm fronds. There were always cigarette butts inside, some dirty words scratched into the wall, and maybe part of a skin magazine.

I don't think one girl had ever been there, but every boy in Norbu went through a time when it was the only place he really wanted to be. Kyle and I brought Pappy once when we were nine or so, and he said it was just about the best hideout he'd ever seen.

Sitting outside, as far apart as humanly possible, were Nigel—who was carefully clipping his toenails—and Paul, a monster kid who must've weighed two hundred pounds. He was in black-and-silver cutoff sweats and a black-and-silver tank top. An L.A. Raiders baseball cap perched on his big head. He was sunk so far into one of the trashed chairs that his arms and legs stuck up in the air like some guy in an inner tube floating on Dirt Lake.

"Where've you been?" he demanded. "I've been stuck here with this major wuss while he picked his toes."

Nigel slipped his nail clippers into a small black case, zipped it up, and tucked it into a brown leather satchel. Then he stood up and brushed at his pale linen shorts. "I think we should get started."

Walter backed his bike until he stood beside Kyle and me. Then he looked up at us expectantly.

"Sure," said Kyle. "Why not."

"Sure," echoed Walter.

"Hold it! Hold it!" Paul heaved himself onto his feet. "I got somethin' to say."

We looked at him. Nigel slipped into some expensive-looking green suede sandals and padded our way.

"So?" I asked finally.

Paul was panting from just standing up. "I think this whole study group thing bites. I just want you all to know that."

"Whatever," said Kyle.

"And I'm real real suspicious of all of you."

"Whatever," echoed Walter.

Puffing, Paul pulled himself upright. "So I got a little test here."

"It's to pass a test," Nigel pointed out, "that we're here. And if you looked around at the other study groups, it's clear that Mr. Wright put the weakest students with the strongest."

"I'm not weak," said Walter.

"I didn't mean you, but the fact is you're a straight-C student."

"So? A C's not weak."

Paul drained the can of Coke he'd been toying with, then crushed the can, the *aluminum* can, and glared at Nigel. "You I don't talk to unless it's absolutely necessary, and I never want you to like touch my food or anything, get it?"

Then he pointed to Kyle and me. "These two," he said, as if a huge audience hung on his every word, "are like married; I never see one without the other." Finally he glanced at Walter. "And then there's Shrimp Delight here."

"I'm not that short!" Walter fumed.

Paul reached under his chair and brought out a peanut butter jar. "So I got this little test, see. There's a certain kind of guy could never pass this test, and I think you know the kind of guy I mean." He opened the jar up and poured four dime-sized frogs onto his big palm. "You take one of these, and hold it in your mouth, okay?"

Nigel inquired mildly, "Why?"

" 'Cause it means you're okay. It means you're a real man."

Kyle grinned at me. "If I'd been born in Africa,

I'd be a prince, and beautiful maidens would bring me delicacies. But oh, no, I'm born in Norbu, California, and some white guy I barely know shoves a Skippy jar full of frogs at me."

"Speaking of Africa," said Nigel, "when I was there with my family, we ate python meat and monkey's brains and ants, so this shouldn't be so hard." Then he reached over, took one of the frogs, and popped it into his mouth.

Paul staggered back a few steps, like he'd been hit by a bakery truck. Kyle and I looked at each other; then Kyle took a couple, one for each of us. As I closed my eyes and dropped mine in, Walter grabbed the last one.

Let me tell you—it was terrible! The frog hopped around in there, ricocheting off my teeth. And if that wasn't bad enough, it tasted like peanut butter. Slimy peanut butter. Man, this was one snack that was not going to replace Chee•tos.

But I kept it in there until Nigel politely let his hop out onto his hand, then squatted down and let it go. So Kyle and I did, too.

Walter, though, coughed, grimaced, squirmed, then beamed up at us. "I did it!" he announced, flexing his thin little arms. "I swallowed mine."

Even Nigel made a face.

"Man, I don't want to even think where you're gonna have warts," said Kyle.

Paul stared at the ground, where the other three frogs were racing away. Then he stared at us. "Far out," he said finally.

Nigel reached into his satchel. "Frogs are a source of protein along the Amazon," he said.

Paul eyed the spick-and-span spiral notebook that Nigel had pulled out. "I wish you were a source of protein along the Amazon, man. You are worse than Mr. Wright."

"I like to be organized."

Paul sank back into his creaking chair, oozing through the spaces between the crisscrossed webbing. The empty frog jar slipped from his hand and rolled away.

"I just want to know enough to not flunk," he said, fanning himself. "I don't want to get sensitive or anything."

"I wouldn't worry about that," I assured him.

"Our novels," Nigel announced, "are *Huckleberry Finn*, *The Grapes of Wrath*, *The Great Gatsby*, *The Last of the Mohicans*, and *Little Women*. An essay from each member of the study group. It can be as short as two pages or as long as five. And we're supposed to help each other."

"How many words is two pages?" Paul asked. "Counting all the *a*'s and *to*'s and periods and stuff."

Walter answered, "A lot, I bet." Then he rubbed his stomach.

"Feelin' a little jumpy?" Kyle asked.

I chimed in. "Feel like sitting on a lily pad?"

Nigel waved the study guide to get our attention. "Let's start out by choosing novels. Who wants *Huckleberry Finn?*"

Walter pointed to Kyle and me. "You guys take it," he screeched. "You're black and white just like Jim and Huck. It's perfect."

"He's kidding, isn't he?" said Kyle.

I shook my head. "No, you really are black."

"That explains a lot, like what I'm doing with black parents. I always wondered."

"All right, all right," Paul said. "What's the difference. I'll take the Huckster."

Nigel moved his gold pen down the page, put a capital *P* beside the first book on the list, then announced, "*Little Women?*"

"Don't look at me," Walter said.

Paul glowered at Nigel. "Yeah, leave him alone. This homie might be on the short side, but he's okay. All you guys did was hold a little frog in your mouth. He ate his." He held up one palm, and Walter eagerly jumped to slap it.

"Since you're so great, Walter," Nigel said, "you and Mr. Gatsby should get along just fine." He made another initial.

Walter just looked pale. "I'm thirsty," he said, holding his stomach, "but I don't want to make a pond for him in there."

Nigel turned to me. "Three left. Which do you

49

want: grapes, Indians, or women?" I was staring at the prints my boots made in the dirt. And when I didn't answer right away, he prompted, "Jesse?"

"Sorry, I was thinking about something. I'll take the Indians."

"What were you thinking about?" asked Walter, sitting down as close as he could and looking right up at me.

"My granddad."

"Why? Is he sick?" Walter stood up. "He didn't forget his horse down at the gas station again, did he?"

"Hey, that only happened one time, okay?"

"So what were you thinking about?"

Kyle ambled over. "Stay tuned," he said, making his voice deep and announcerlike, "for further adventures of Walter Brown, District Attorney. He asks the questions polite people won't ask."

"Yeah, butt out, Walter." I took a deep breath. "Pappy just made a little mistake."

"What mistake?" Walter asked.

I reached for him with both hands, like the mad strangler, as Kyle laced his arm around my shoulders and pulled me away.

"Wait a minute," he said. "Maybe you should just go ahead and tell him. We could use these guys. If all five of us go up there and comb every inch of the place, then Pappy can't say to you, 'We missed something.' Right?"

"I guess." I glanced over my shoulder and half whispered, "But then three more guys know, and in Norbu that means pretty soon a hundred people know, and one of those is my mom!"

Walter burrowed between Kyle and me. "No way, no way. I wouldn't tell a soul. Nobody would. We'll make a bloody pact by moonlight. Anybody who breaks it dies by fire." He squirmed free. "Paul, you got a pocketknife?"

"Hey, I'm not cuttin' anything. I don't even know what the secret is."

I sighed. "It's not that big a deal. Pappy and I were just, uh, up in the Santa Rios this morning, and Pappy thinks he saw this old paw print, so I've gotta take him back tomorrow so he knows for sure it's just, you know, what it is and not a . . ." I couldn't make myself say it.

"A what?" asked Paul.

I mumbled something.

"A what?" asked Walter.

They were all looking at me, so I said it. "Tiger track, okay? Pappy thinks he might have seen a tiger track."

Walter jumped up. "Are you kidding?"

"Hey, hey. Relax. It's not a tiger track. It can't be. But I've got to get that story out of his head before he blabs to Mom."

"But if there was a tiger, we could trap him!" Paul exclaimed. "Get our picture in the paper."

"For sure!" Walter, frog-powered, started bouncing all over the place. "We could make him a mascot. Take him to school on a leash."

"Guys," Kyle said, "relax. There's no tiger."

"Did you see it?" demanded Walter.

"No, but just because it's as hot as India around here, it's not India, and there aren't any tigers," Kyle answered.

He turned to me. "Did you see it?"

"No, but . . ."

"My dad told me," Walter said, "that Pappy is the best tracker and cowboy and outdoorsman he ever saw."

"Look, Pappy's great at that stuff, but anybody can make a mistake. He probably saw some poor old thirsty mountain lion's print and got excited. But that isn't even the point. The point is that if Mom hears about it, there's gonna be trouble. He slips one little bit, and she's packing his bag for old Golden Arteries."

"Perhaps your mother is right. He might need a controlled environment. There is a kind of dementia peculiar to older—"

Kyle and I said it together: "Shut up, Nigel."

"Let's just go look," said Walter. "What's it gonna hurt to look?"

"I'll go," said Paul, "if I don't have to hike."

"I'll ask if you can ride one of my dad's dirt bikes!" Walter cried.

"Kickin'! I'm in."

Walter turned to the rest of us. "We could be like a gang," he said. "We could call ourselves the Savage Avengers. And have secret names like Viper, Gargantua, and Thunderbolt. And we'd always talk in code. Like for *book* we'd say *beans*. So we see each other in the hall, okay? And I say like, 'What's happening, Viper? Read any good beans lately?' And then Viper would say, 'Cornflakes,' which would mean yes."

Kyle turned to me. "There's still time to make a run for it. This could be contagious."

I ran my hands through my hair. "You're the one who wanted 'em in on it, remember?"

Walter looked over at Nigel. "Will you come, too?"

Nigel waited a second or two. "I've actually seen tiger tracks," he said. "When we were in India."

"Are they big?" Walter asked. "Really big?"

"Uh-huh."

"Well," I muttered, "you're not gonna see any in Norbu."

Paul said, "I'm not campin' out, though. I don't like beans, and people who camp out always eat beans."

"So we'll bring some Pop-Tarts," said Kyle. "Right now I need a book, Nigel."

"Well, if you'll take Steinbeck, I'll take Alcott."

"Fine with me."

Nigel stood up then and swung his satchel over one shoulder. "And as for tigers, let's say two o'clock at my house?"

The next afternoon, after all the chores were done, I went out and saddled Marky Mark, looking him over first like Pappy had taught me: feeling his legs for heat and patting him down good for ticks and stuff like that. Then I rode over to meet Kyle, who was saddled up but talking to his dad in the driveway.

Marcus McDaniel had an old Dodge double-wide with a chrome trailer hitch. It could pull a dozen of the Brangus cattle that he raised and sold. On the door, written at an angle, were the words BAR NONE RANCH, which was no joke because Mr. McDaniel would hire anybody—any age or color or gender—who worked hard and was honest.

Kyle's father waved when I reined up by the water trough, slid off Marky Mark, and walked their way.

Mr. McDaniel—dressed like always in polished boots, pressed jeans, and a white shirt—looked down at the book Kyle was holding.

"What's that you're reading now?" His voice seemed to rumble up from underground.

"Oh, jeez," said Kyle. "You caught me. I know I

promised I wouldn't read anymore, and I know how much it cost to send me to Readers' Rehab, but you don't know what it's like."

He dropped the book and clutched at his dad's arm. "I think I'm fine, you know? I think I'm strong. And then I hit the streets and there's guys everywhere sellin' nonfiction, biography, and—God help me—poetry. And before I know it, I've got my nose in a book again."

He pretended to sob, leaning into his father's big arm. "Don't tell Mom, please. She'll be so disappointed."

Mr. McDaniel got his son in a harmless headlock and shook him good a couple of times. Then he looked at me. "I don't know if you're a bad influence on him or if he's a bad influence on you."

"Mom can't figure it out either."

He climbed into his truck. "Say hi to Pappy for me."

"Yes, sir."

I watched the big truck back toward the spotless double garage, then pull away and head for the ranch, just a few miles down the road. Kyle—wearing a T-shirt with ARRESTED DEVELOPMENT on the front—slipped the hitch and led Surfer Boy across the immaculate driveway.

As I reached up and patted the palomino's pale nose, Kyle asked, "Where is Pappy, anyway?"

"He said he'd meet us up there. I put notes on the toilet seat, the refrigerator, the back door, and his horse; so wherever he goes, he gets reminded."

"He didn't blow it with your mom and start talking tiger at breakfast?"

I shook my head. "As far as Mom's concerned, this is just another camping trip. She only made me promise to stay really close to him, like always. Said she didn't get why we wanted to go back to where we'd been, but I told her she didn't understand real men, and she said that was the truth."

That made us both grin, so we mounted up, clucked to our horses simultaneously, and headed for the street.

"Wasn't that a weird scene at the cave yesterday?" Kyle asked.

"Yeah. It's funny to go to school with those guys and say hi to 'em and all, but not really know them until you, like, have to." I leaned into Marky's neck, brushing his stiff mane all to one side.

"Paul called me last night. Said he was starting on his paper and wanted to know if a huckleberry was pretty much the same thing as a strawberry."

"So what's his essay—'Fruit and the Classic American Novel'?"

"Aw, Paul's okay," Kyle said. "Kind of what you'd expect: big guy dressed like a Raiders wannabe."

"Nigel's the strange one."

"Yeah. I tried talkin' to him when he showed up a couple of months ago, but he just blew me off."

I nodded. "In the newspaper it said his dad was famous. All kinds of prizes for his photographs and stuff, but the one they printed was gross—just some dead zebra with flies all over it."

Kyle fiddled with the cord that held his hat on, sliding the red bead up and down. "Maybe Nigel is just kind of permanently chilled, you know? Who'd want to get tight with a new bunch of guys every year and then say *adiós*?"

I looked over at Kyle, whose old cowboy hat—black with red plastic trim wound around the brim—now hung down his back.

"If he needs a best friend, maybe I could let him have you. For a price."

Kyle winced and grabbed at his chest, pretending to be wounded. "That hurts." Suddenly he looked straight up, eyes narrowed. "What's that?"

I fell for it. "Where?"

And Kyle was gone, leaning into Surfer Boy's mane, his "I'll race you!" hanging in the air behind him.

The house that Nigel's parents had leased stood pretty much by itself toward the end of an unpaved road. Kyle beat me to it by half a length; then we both galloped out another hundred yards or so before turning around and jogging back.

We tied the horses up, then slipped past a beat-up

four-wheeled ATV that belonged to Walter's dad. It stood in the driveway beside a stripped-down dirt bike, which might have been a Harley once but was so patched together it was more like some kind of mechanical quilt. Then there was Nigel's dad's leased maroon Dynasty, as dirty as a field car.

I knocked on the big phony door, which was laminated and painted to look like something out of California's colorful past.

Nigel's mom opened it; she was wrapped in what looked like aluminum foil, and she resembled a baked potato. I guess we were staring, because she laughed and said, "Fashionwise, this is the latest thing. Keeps you cool in the summer, warm in the winter."

"And," Kyle said out of the side of his mouth, "if you stand outside you get cable."

I gave him an elbow where it would do the most good.

"Call me Maureen." She held out her hand, and we took turns shaking it. Then she pointed. "Everybody's in here."

We trailed her across the cool, red tiles—heavy plastic ones that came scarred to look like the real thing. Maureen's hair was coal-mine black, cut so short it looked like a cap. She wore little gold slippers with turned-up, harem-type toes. A tape measure hung around her neck and a little red pincushion decorated her left wrist.

Just before she stepped aside and pointed us into the living room, she whirled and said earnestly, "I'm so glad to finally meet Nigel's friends." She grabbed my hand and Kyle's. "I've been begging him to bring his friends home."

"Well," said Kyle quickly, "school takes up a lot of time, and . . ." He ran one hand over his close-cropped hair nervously, so I tried to help out.

". . . and there's lots to do in Norbu."

"Well, never mind," Maureen said. "You're all here now, and I want a picture. I'm going to go get Thomas."

After she'd hurried away, Kyle turned to me. "Lots to do in Norbu?"

"Well, you were stuck."

"Hey, I would've thought of something better than 'lots to do in Norbu.' "

"At least it rhymed."

Kyle grabbed me around the neck and we half-heartedly wrestled our way down a couple of stairs and into the living room, where Walter and Paul were watching a huge color TV.

Kyle took a look around and let me slip out of his headlock. "Wow."

There were wicker couches and chairs and, on wicker end tables, big cacti with black stones filling up the pots. Huge brass candlesticks loomed over the tiled coffee table, and barbed wire coiled artistically around the base of each one. Sleigh bells stitched to leather straps hung on every door, and rusty spurs older than Pappy hung from the fireplace.

"This place," I whispered, "makes me feel like I live in a bunkhouse."

"You do. Your mom's apartment is nice, but you and Pappy pretty much do live in a bunkhouse."

"Oh, well, no wonder."

There were framed photographs of Maureen and Nigel everywhere: her leaning into a pool and kissing a dolphin. Nigel on skis wearing a red parka. Both of them by a hut with a bunch of little guys holding blowguns.

"Did they really do all this stuff," Kyle asked, "or have they been cloned?"

I gave him a shove and he staggered over to the couch just as Paul, holding the remote at arm's length like a ray gun, started around the channels.

"Wait!" Walter pawed at Paul's big hand. "I love the Roadrunner."

Paul stared as Wile E. Coyote fell from a cliff, then picked himself up and started to unpack still another contraption from a huge carton.

"He never gets what he wants," Paul said. "That always bothered me." He turned toward Kyle and me. "Does that bother you guys?"

"That's good thinking," Nigel said, coming into the room from a narrow door by the bookshelves. "That kind of insight on your essay could get you an A."

Paul frowned. "What would I do with an A?"

I took in Nigel's blue shorts, ironed T-shirt, long-billed hat with flaps on the back, and tall lace-up boots as Paul pinched the remote; a golf course flashed past, then an angry cowboy, two crying flight attendants, and an infomercial for knives so sharp they could cut other knives. He stopped at girls in Jell-O–colored outfits gyrating on platforms and stairs. Couples waved their arms wildly like they were the smartest kids in school and couldn't wait to answer.

Paul reached around and offered a plateful of green things to Kyle and me. "Nigel's mom brought 'em in before."

I asked what they were. " 'Cause if they're not square and made out of Rice Krispies, I'm lost."

Paul shoveled a couple down. "Dunno. I've been trying to figure that out."

Kyle took one. "Couldn't be worse than a frog."

Just then Maureen appeared in the door and announced, "Photo opportunity!" as Nigel's dad followed her into the room.

"Gentlemen," he said with a smile, "my name is Thomas," and he dutifully shook all our hands.

"We saw you," said Kyle, "at the ostrich races."

"Right. That part was nonsense, but I got some great character shots." He looked at himself in the nearest smoky mirror. "They were worth the trip downtown, 'cause that's what I'm after: the kinds of faces that stand for a whole way of life that's just disappearing."

"My granddad," I blurted, "versus Bobby Yates."

Nigel's dad looked at me, *really* looked at me. "Very good," he said. "I might be able to use that."

"So you know Pappy?"

"He's that old cowboy with the ponytail, right? Yes, I've talked to him. Got his picture the first week we were in Norbu."

Maureen began to shoo us toward the fireplace like she was herding calves, and we milled around uneasily as she closed in. Nigel, slipping between Kyle and me, whispered, "It's easier to cooperate. It'll be over in a minute."

We stood in front of a huge Oriental carpet that had been framed and hung on the wall. Thomas sighted through one of half a dozen gadgets either hanging from his neck or from some Velcro strap.

"Hope he gets the light perfect," I whispered to Kyle, "so every zit shows."

Nigel's dad took about five pictures, then moved us around and clicked off four or five more. As Maureen wrote down our names, Walter announced, "All together we're called the Savage Avengers."

Thomas smiled. "Duly noted." Then he snapped the case on an expensive-looking Nikon, shook our hands once more, and left with his arm around his wife's shoulders.

As Paul fell back onto the couch again, he said, "Wow, so these are your dad's books."

I watched him lean toward the coffee table, then deal them out like giant playing cards. He read the names half out loud—*"Farewell to Africa, The Disappearing South, Last Days of an Empire."*

Walter stared at the nearest cover, which featured a tall, gaunt black man with the deepest, saddest eyes I've ever seen. "My dad says that's why your dad's here. We're on the way out, too."

"Well, it's not like it's his fault," snapped Nigel. "It already happened. He just takes pictures of it."

"I didn't say it was his fault. All I said was—"

"Hey, are we going to argue or go tiger hunting?" Paul demanded.

"My Kawasaki's out back," Nigel muttered. "Meet you in a second."

A few minutes later we rode out over land so bone dry it cracked. Kyle and I let the others go ahead. Our horses were used to cars and motorbikes and all, but that didn't mean they liked the noise or the smell.

Paul was big enough to make the tires of the little Honda ATV half flatten out, and Walter zipped around him on his motorbike like a pesky insect. Nigel rode just behind them on a superclean 250 cc Kawasaki, most of the time with both of his feet out like training wheels.

Kyle wiped his forehead. "Where's Pappy going to meet us?"

"Just beyond the switchbacks."

He looked up, squinting, took a drink out of his canteen, and poured a little along Surfer Boy's neck. Then he narrowed his eyes. "Maybe I better not waste that," he growled. "We're goin' to Satan's Sandbox, the driest spot in the universe. Why, I've seen guys kill for a drop of cool, clear water up there."

"Really?" I said. "You've seen them kill?"

"Well, maybe not, but I've seen them get peeved and throw things."

I laughed as we wound our way through some piñon trees and scrub oak and rode without saying anything for a little while. Horseback riding looks easy, but it takes leg muscles and balance. Pappy had showed me ways to help a horse climb and just make things easier for him in general. Marky Mark, who'd been tossing his mane and playing around on the flat, put his head down and started to lather up.

About twenty minutes later, leaving the others behind while Walter tinkered with an engine, Kyle and I came to a wide place in the trail next to a couple of huge boulders lodged in a notch. Locals called this the Gunsight.

Pappy was slumped in his saddle. Cody had his head down, too, and a neighbor's old packhorse—

carrying sleeping bags, a tarp, and some gear—was leaning on a smooth rock face.

"If Nigel's dad was here," said Kyle, "he'd take a picture and call it *The Last Roundup*."

"Well, I wouldn't let him, okay? He's just asleep. It's not the last anything."

"Hey, easy, cuz."

I jumped off Marky, walked right over to Pappy, and shook him gently. When he swung down off his horse, the saddle slipped sideways a little, and I noticed he'd forgotten his saddle blanket, the one we'd bought in Cambria, the one that was just like mine. So I asked him where it was.

"Why, it's on the horse's back, Jesse."

I patted Cody. "Not this horse."

My granddad started looking around like he'd dropped a quarter.

"It didn't just fall off. You must have forgot it."

"Here it is!" Kyle yelled from the other side of the packhorse, then tossed the soft blanket to me. "He packed it with the ice. Tell me this doesn't mean he's been riding on my steak."

As Pappy scratched his head and frowned and I got Cody saddled right, the other guys pulled up.

Paul switched off his engine. His voice was loud, like he was still talking over the noise. "And tell me somethin' else. This *Huckleberry Finn*'s about freedom, okay?"

"Okay." Nigel sounded suspicious.

"Then it don't make sense to me to sit in a hot little classroom and go on and on about freedom."

"Good. Write about that," Nigel urged.

"What? Write about what?"

"The paradox."

Paul looked our way.

"A paradox is like a pair of pants," Kyle said.

"But smaller," I added.

As Nigel patiently leaned forward to reason with Paul, Pappy asked, "These your new sidekicks?"

"The Savage Avengers," said Kyle. "A ruthless gang of eighth-grade English students."

"Some have been late to class." I pretended to shudder. "And Walter wrote in a library book once."

I walked Pappy over to the others and he shook hands with Paul and Nigel. "I know Walter. We hang out together at the Dairy Queen sometimes."

"Just say *hang*, Pappy. Nobody says *hang out* anymore."

"And Walter's teachin' me slang." Pappy grinned, then excused himself and disappeared behind a boulder.

Paul shaded his eyes and looked up at the switchbacks. "Is the old guy gonna be okay?" he asked.

"He can outride you any day," I snapped.

"Yeah," said Kyle. "Just worry about getting your own butt up there."

Paul held up both hands, palms out. He wore black weight-lifter's gloves, so his fingers looked white as candles. "Jeez, take it easy. I didn't mean anything."

"All right!" Pappy appeared, buttoning the fly of his Levi's. "Let's go find us a tiger."

I looked over at Kyle and muttered, "He forgets his pills, his boots, and where he lives. But will he forget a paw print that probably came from some poor lost dog? Oh, no."

Walter crowed, "I think there's a tiger up there, too, Pappy. I dreamed about it last night."

My grandfather turned Walter's rally cap around, setting it straight on his head. Then he waved in the direction their bikes were already headed. "Now, you boys with the noisy motors give us a head start. We're aiming toward Colton."

Just then Walter pointed. "Look at this!"

We all watched a single feather spiral down and land at his feet.

"A good sign," said Pappy.

"That makes the second one today. This mornng my birthday was the same as the lost kid on the milk carton. And now this." Walter held the feather up, letting the sun play off it as he searched the sky.

Pappy ran two fingers over it lightly. "Did you boys know there's Indians whose craft is workin' with feathers?"

"Indian girls?" Paul said.

Pappy shook his head. "Warriors. And some of them work most of a lifetime and never measure up to eagle feathers."

"How do you mean 'measure up'?" asked Nigel.

"Just that. They're not worthy and they know it. Eagle's a powerful symbol for an Indian. Say you kill an eagle just to dress yourself up in his feathers so you can go courtin'. Why, a gal would just run the other way."

"How would she know?" asked Kyle.

Pappy touched his chest. "She just would. And if you'd done the same thing so's you could look like a warrior? Why, a little guy with humble feathers on his belt, say from a coot, maybe, would just kick your behind good."

I watched my grandfather drag his gray ponytail over one shoulder. I liked hearing this story again. His voice was firm and his eyes had gotten brighter.

"Need to be careful," Pappy said, "about shootin' things. Animals got rights, too." Then he handed Walter the feather. "Be careful with this, son."

Just then Paul started up the ATV he was strad-dling, and the horses shook their heads and pranced. "Let's boogie!" he shouted, planting his feet and hauling the two front wheels of the Honda up in the air. "Kickin'!" he bellowed. "Tigers come out from everywhere to watch the champ grab serious air."

"Where'd you find him?" Pappy asked, putting a cigarette together as we rode past.

"We drew him in a lottery."

Pappy grinned. "Was he first prize or last?"

The three of us rode for a quarter of a mile or so. We could hear the sound of the others' engines fading away, then drifting toward us again. As we got farther from town, it got drier, if that was possible. The manzanita didn't even look red anymore. I remembered riding around these hills when the smell of field mint under the horse's hooves nearly made my eyes water. Now the discouraged-looking chokeberry trees showed where the water used to be, but wasn't now and hadn't been for a long time.

I clucked to Marky Mark and pulled up even with Pappy, who pinched his cigarette out, then field-stripped it.

"Jesse," he asked, "did I take my medicine?"

"Uh-huh. 'Cause afterward I locked it up."

"Why'd you do that?"

"Because you might forget and take it again."

He scratched his head and tried, I guess, to remember that he forgot things. Then he dismounted and went behind another boulder.

"I wish Mom could have heard him tell that story about the eagle feathers. He didn't miss a beat."

Pretty soon the others came putting up. Immediately Pappy started to sweep the dry hills through his binoculars.

I looked at Kyle and we both shook our heads when we heard Paul say to Nigel, "How can it be so"—he raised two fingers on each hand to show quotation marks—" 'relevant'? Hucks runs away from home, right? And it's all hunky-dory, right? Well, if I ran away from home, the cops'd be after me, and I'd end up talking to the school shrink."

"So write about that. Say it's *not* relevant. Mr. Wright wants to know what you think."

Paul shook his head. "No, no, no. Teachers want to hear what *they* think."

"Mr. Wright's not like that."

"Hey, it's not his fault or anything. That's just school."

Below us lay what was left of the man-made reservoir that'd once covered up the little town of Colton. But when the drought got really bad, the branch of the Sticks River that fed the reservoir dried up; and as the water receded, the town emerged again, little by little, like a huge photo developing from the edges first. Shacks poked their roofs out, then their windows. A fence appeared, a street, a store or two, the stone circle of a well, and hitching posts. Where fish had swum among old tables and chairs, weekenders roamed in their yellow L. L. Bean boots, looking for old bottles and coal-oil lanterns.

Now it was deserted, picked clean.

"Coal Town stinks," said Paul. "I been down there. There's nothin'."

Kyle leaned away from Surfer Boy to spit. "Know

why they call it Coal Town? 'Cause mostly black people used to live there."

"Really?" asked Nigel, looking doubtful.

Pappy agreed with Kyle. "Real name's Colton. I used to cowboy with a fella who lived there."

I shaded my eyes. It was Sunday, but the place was empty. Tire tracks crisscrossed the boggy edges, and off to the north cattle came down to drink. One of them wandered up toward a porch like he'd been invited to sit down.

Kyle leaned back in the saddle. "My dad said that when the state wanted to bring water in, they picked this place for the reservoir because the blacks couldn't do anything about it."

"People's more shortsighted than they used to be," Pappy said. "They'll take any old quick fix. Kick people out that's lived somewhere for years. Bleed the land dry tryin' to squeeze one more cash crop out of it." Then he pointed. "And it's a cryin' shame about the old Sticks here. Rivers don't like to be dammed up and have to stand still. Now, rainwater will collect, and that's different, but a river wants to get on with it." He shook his head.

"It's just a river," said Paul. "It's not like it's got feelings or anything."

"I wonder," Pappy said to nobody in particular. Then he turned to Paul. "You think animals have feelings, son?"

Paul looked down at the gauges in front of him. "Yeah, I guess. Not like people, though."

"Big Bad John was really mad yesterday," Walter informed us. "He told me so right after the race."

"Couldn't bring myself to see that spectacle," said my grandfather. "Seemed humiliating."

"To Bobby?" Kyle asked.

"Oh, probably. But I was thinking of them poor birds." He felt for his tobacco, then just left his hand over his heart. "When I was younger, I shot animals for meat and sometimes for sport, I admit that. But the older I get, the more I think how they must feel about things. Guess you could say I identify with the beasts somehow."

He stretched, looking straight up at the sun for a second. "I get more like 'em every day: I like to eat good, then go to sleep. Like to feel a breeze. Like to get away from people. So there's no way I could watch an ostrich in a saddle. It'd be disrespectful." Then he handed Kyle the binoculars. "Those your dad's cattle down there?"

Kyle took a while to answer. Like the rest of us, he was probably thinking over what Pappy had said.

"Uh, no," he said finally. "Bobby Yates has got a few Brangus now, but naturally he wouldn't want what Dad's got, so he bought himself some of the red ones from the Texas strain."

I took the binoculars. "They don't look filled out

like your dad's. Maybe Bobby doesn't measure up to working with Brangus, huh? Maybe he ought to start with hamsters."

Kyle grinned.

Pappy winked at me as he turned to Walter. "Let's go see our tiger print."

"Mountain lion," I said automatically.

Pretty soon we all pulled up under a couple of dead-looking eucalyptus, and Pappy pointed.

"Up and over there. And let's climb on foot for a time. We about made enough noise this trip."

Panting, planting our boots sideways for traction, we all got to within fifty yards of where Granddad and I had camped; then we slumped in the shade of a monument-sized piece of rock.

"It's easier comin' up the other side." He jerked his thumb to the west. "But this way the wind's not gonna carry our scent down and scare old mister mountain lion." He bore down on the last couple of words, then looked my way. "All right?"

"Thank you."

Paul was red-faced and wheezing. "This is worse than the stadium stairs by a million times," he said, spitting out the sentence in bits and pieces like it tasted bad. He drained his canteen and took Pappy's when it was offered.

"This here," Pappy said between breaths, "is limestone." He slapped the rock face. "Only limestone for fifty miles. How'd it get here?"

Nigel, perched on a rock, ventured, "Movement of the lithospheric plates?"

"Somethin' big, that's for sure," Pappy said, pointing north, "to make this slide all the way down here from all the way up there."

Paul groaned and rubbed his red knees. "So what?"

"Just puts things in perspective, sort of. For me, anyhow. Makes my own problems seem about as big as a gnat."

I manufactured a grin. "You don't have any problems, Granddad."

"Maybe not." He turned to Walter. "Let's you and me, and whoever wants to, slither up to that rise there and see what's what." He handed over the binoculars. "Take these, okay? You got young eyes."

Walter, looking pleased, raised up warily. He licked one finger and tested the wind. Then he nodded. "All clear," he rasped.

"I'm not goin' one more step," Paul exclaimed. "That tiger can just come to me."

"Mountain lion!" I insisted.

Nigel waved them on, too. "And I've seen a lot of tigers."

Kyle lay down. "I've never seen a tiger, but I've seen Nigel, who's seen a tiger. That's close enough for me."

I followed my granddad and Walter to the top of the ridge, then plopped down between them. The Yateses' big ranch started right at the leeward side of the little peak we were perched on. It wasn't green by a long shot, but it wasn't as brown as the rest of the county, either. The protected trees grew straighter and the chokeberry didn't lean hardly at all.

Pappy stood staring at the ground. "It was right about here."

I leaned down for a closer look, then started moving around slowly, like somebody who's lost a contact lens.

"All I see is horse tracks," said Walter.

"Me, too," Pappy said. "Jesse, I don't remember all these the other day, do you?"

"Maybe they're from you guys' horses," Walter guessed.

"These are from old shoes," I said, shaking my head and pointing. "They're slick and run down in the back. Pappy wouldn't let Cody out of the corral with shoes half this bad."

Walter wandered in bigger and bigger circles. Then he got down on all fours, his behind up in the air like one of those drag racers on ESPN. Finally he shouted, "Here!"

Sure enough, in some loose dirt right beside a rock were some paw prints.

Pappy squatted down, then fell back onto his butt before he could steady himself. He pushed away the hand I offered and got up on his own.

"Mountain lion," he said. "Young one. But that ain't the print I saw."

"Are you sure?" whined Walter.

"Sure I'm sure." Then he took off his hat. "Is it hot out here, Jesse? I'm hot."

"Only about a hundred and two, Granddad."

He pointed to the east side of a big rock. "I'll be over here." Even before I could ask, he added, "And I'm all right. I'm just hot."

Walter and I watched him settle down in the shade; then Walter whispered, "Is this really a mountain lion's footprint?"

"Uh-huh."

"How does he know it's a young one?"

" 'Cause it's not very deep, you know? A young cat doesn't weigh as much as an old one."

Walter looked down at the print. "It couldn't be anything else?"

"Besides a mountain lion, you mean? Probably not. It's not a bobcat, 'cause . . . well, look here." I pointed to another set of tracks. "A bobcat's walking gait is real tight 'cause his legs are short. These here are pretty far away, just right for a young puma."

"But not a tiger."

"I never saw a tiger track and neither did Pappy, but you know they'd be big." I pointed down again.

"But I've seen a lot of these, and this is a mountain lion."

Walter looked up at me as I wiped my dusty hands on my pants. "Did Pappy teach you all this?" he asked.

"Uh-huh. But not like school or anything. We'd just go for a ride and he'd point things out. I remember when I was little I thought there was nothing going on up here and I'd kind of want to go back to town. But he'd start showing me stuff and pretty soon he had me making up stories."

"What kind of stories?"

"Oh, you know, a deer's print is kind of heart-shaped, and you could follow 'em if the ground was damp, and then there'd be this like commotion and the way the hooves hit the ground'd change. So he'd have me look around, and there'd be some big cat's prints, and the story was that the deer was just nosing along and he almost got killed, but he was fast enough and lucky enough to get away."

Walter rubbed his arms like he was, of all things, cold. "I wish my dad had taught me this stuff instead of how to tear down an engine."

"That's not a bad thing to know, Walter."

"Hey, you fellas. Come look at this!"

We started for Pappy, who was standing about twenty yards above us.

"What?" Walter screamed. "Do you see the tiger?"

77

Pappy, grinning, motioned for the binoculars.

"John!" Walter bellowed, waving with one hand. "Big Bad John!"

"The ostrich?" I said.

"Uh-huh. Guess I forgot to tell you. A partner of mine called this morning to gab. Said some guy in Osco bought the other three but wanted nothin' to do with the fourth one. Bobby had to carry him on home and turn him out."

I pried the glasses away from Walter. "So now Bobby's got a psycho ostrich roaming his land?"

Twenty minutes later, we were back with the others. Walter told about seeing the print and then about the ostrich. Toward the end, he got that dreamy look again, the one where he cocked one ear and his mouth hung open. "John says he's not psycho," he reported. "He's just mad at Bobby."

"It's just a matter of time, isn't it," whispered Kyle, "and Walter's on the cover of the *Enquirer*." When I laughed, he asked, "So for sure no tiger?"

"Nah, just some old prints from a puma, and not a very big one, either."

"Pappy's pretty hard to fool with this outdoors stuff."

I looked over at my granddad, who was fussing

with Cody. Then I half whispered to Kyle, "Well, he got fooled this time."

Just then Walter started his bike, revved it way up, and made it jump forward like a nervous horse.

Paul straddled his ATV. "See you dudes around."

Nigel glided up beside Pappy. "I'll bet my dad ought to do more than just get your picture. Would it be all right if he brought a tape recorder and talked to you?"

Pappy dug into the front pocket of his green shirt.

Nigel persisted. "Would it?"

Pappy looked puzzled. "Would what?"

I stepped up beside my grandfather. "Anytime," I told Nigel. "Anytime your dad wants." Then I looked at the others. "Now, are you guys goin' or what? We got to find a place to camp."

As Pappy looked around, blinking and frowning, Paul, Nigel, and Walter putted away, leaving a blue haze behind them.

"You want to lie down, Pappy?" I asked.

"You boys tired, are you?"

"I could rest, couldn't you, Kyle?"

"Sure."

I hurried over to the packhorse, slipped the half hitch, and let the thin sleeping bags tumble to the ground. I pitched Kyle his underhanded, and carried the other two into the shade of the granite boulder.

"Run a stick up under there," Pappy said, pointing, "in case some old rattler's takin' himself a siesta where it's cool."

I rattled a dry manzanita limb, then spread out my grandfather's sleeping bag, opening the checkered side all the way out. Then I propped up against the rock as Kyle rustled through a backpack, taking out chips, another canteen, and some paperback books.

"Hungry, Pappy?" Kyle asked, rattling the cellophane bag.

Pappy shook his head and tugged his boots off. He had one black sock and one gray one. Then he lay back with a sigh.

"Want some water, Granddad?" I asked.

"Just thinkin' about things." He half rolled toward us. "Remember when you and me was down by that relocation center right at the start of the war, and that little Johansen girl was sayin' good-bye to a Japanese boy, and she had to put her arms through the wire like this here to hug him?" Arms out, he said to the sky, "Remember?"

Oh, man. "Sure, Pappy."

Kyle stepped in. "Uh, Mr. Wright showed us pictures of those camps. He said it was a national disgrace."

I reached over and put my hand on Kyle's arm, meaning he could stop now. "He's asleep."

"That was fast."

I took a hard look at my grandfather. Being

around Pappy lately was a little like riding through a forest: trees, trees, trees, trees, trees—then suddenly a clearing, a space, nothing. Then pretty soon trees again.

I watched the old man's chest rise and fall. I took in the weathered neck, the gray stubble on his cheeks, the way his lower lip trembled.

"Sometimes it's like somebody's got one of those TV remotes and he just clicks Pappy onto another channel."

"The Nostalgia Channel."

"Right. It drives Mom nuts. But, really, what's the difference? He's not hurting anybody."

"Does he know when it happens?"

"Sometimes. He told me once it was like all of a sudden bein' in a whole other country. He said just think of the money he saves on travel expenses."

Just then Pappy snorted and sat straight up, looking around wide-eyed. "Had a dream," he said, even before I could ask. " 'Bout a blizzard. I was carryin' these little calves that hadn't mothered up right." He rubbed his arms and stood up. "Whew. Can still hear 'em bawl." Then he stepped into his boots and wandered off, fumbling with the steel buttons on his Levi's.

I watched him carefully. When he'd disappeared, I turned and lay back, squirming comfortably into the cool dirt. "It's nice up here, isn't it?" I said, looking around.

"It's great. We should come up all the time once we're out of school. Just bring stuff to eat and hang with Pappy." Kyle took a deep breath and let it out slowly. "Remember that smog last year when we went to L.A. with my dad?"

"Yeah. There's nothin' to see in Norbu, but at least you can see it."

Kyle fiddled with his hat. He ran his fingers around the brim, which was decorated with a few beads.

"Mom wants me to wear one of those African jobs, you know? They're like woven and real colorful and stuff. How do you think I'd look?"

I glanced behind me. "Where's Pappy now?"

Kyle put his hat back on. "You go see. I'll get the fire started. I'm hungry."

I ambled away, rounded a smoothed-off corner of granite, and stared out at twenty acres of the jumbled, odd-sized boulders that people called the Devil's Playground. But no Pappy.

I yelled for him, thinking he was still buttoning up his pants, but nobody answered. I looked back toward the camp. I checked where the horses were tied. No sign of him. The palms of my hands got damp.

"God, take it easy," I said out loud. "Pappy wouldn't panic. He'd just hunker down and take a look around." And it helped to do just that, still panting and clammy, but not so nuts.

I blinked hard, and wiped my sunglasses clean with a corner of my T-shirt. *Think, Jesse.* There were maybe three ways he could've gone, but which way was the right one? All of them started on busted-up shale and then disappeared among the boulders.

I stood up and yelled for Kyle, and he came running, his hat blown back off his head and dangling from the braided cord.

"What's wrong? Are you okay?" He was leaning on both knees, out of breath.

"Pappy's gone."

"Oh, man. Did you yell for him?"

"Sort of."

"Well, let's really do it." He cupped both hands around his mouth, gave a little one-two-three-go, and we bellowed.

A few birds exploded from somewhere, but that was all.

"God," I said, "I hope he's not lyin' somewhere with a broken leg."

"Want to try once more?" Kyle asked, panting.

I shook my head. "Let's split up." I pointed at what looked like the widest trail. "You go down there. Look for some dirt between the rocks. If you don't see any boot prints at all, come on back."

"All right."

"We gotta find him, and when we do, it's just between you and me, okay? Nobody else has to know this happened."

"Okay, sure." He slapped at my hand and we separated.

The first trail I tried hooked north just after I rounded a barn-sized boulder. I could see pretty well then, but I kept on anyway, until a dry streambed showed me nothing had been through there for days but rabbits.

Kyle was back, too, shaking his head and looking at the third—and last—trail.

"What if he's not there?" he asked.

"He will be. He's gotta be."

Five long minutes later I pointed: first a broken branch here, then a kicked-over rock there. Those led us to a dim path, where I saw fresh heel marks in the smooth dust.

We picked up speed then, sliding over boulders, scrambling and half falling, until I saw his white hat, exactly like mine. He was peering off to the west, one hand shielding his eyes.

"Pappy!" I yelled. "Pappy! Over here."

He turned around, squinted, then waved as we sprinted his way.

"I'm glad to see you boys. I kind of got turned around."

Kyle and I were panting hard. "Where were you goin'?" Kyle asked.

He scratched his head. "I thought I knew once, but I guess I forgot. Figured if I could find Cody, he'd just carry me someplace I could get my bearings."

"Pappy!" I said. "Cody's with us." I pointed over one shoulder. "Back there where we were gonna camp. You came out here with Kyle and me and the other kids."

"Other kids?" he said with a frown. "I don't have any other kids besides Bonnie."

It just killed me to see him standing there like somebody with a loose rope in his hands who knows there was something important at the other end but can't remember what.

I charged right up to him then. "If you go walkin' away like that again and Mom finds out, you're history. We'll never go camping. We'll never do *anything* together." Then all of a sudden I wanted to cry. "You're gonna ruin everything. You have to quit it, Pappy. Quit forgetting stuff. Please!"

I had a tough couple of days after that. I took to waking up in the middle of the night and creeping across the hall to check on Pappy because I was afraid, I guess, that he'd get lost even in his dreams.

So when the three of us set out for Kyle's mom's party, I wasn't in the best shape. We were a little late and had to park way down the street in the dark.

As we walked toward the lights and the music, Mom whispered to me, "Keep an eye on Pappy tonight. I don't want him wandering away from the party."

"He doesn't wander," I lied. "He's just not in a rut like everybody else."

"Oh, sure." She glanced over her shoulder. "What's he doing now?"

"I'll get him."

I hurried back to my granddad, who was leaning

into a rosebush somebody'd managed to keep alive. I could see the big white blooms, like distant explosions, even in the dark.

"You comin'?" I asked.

"Sure. I was just stoppin' to smell the flowers. That's what the song says to do, but when you do it, people think you're crazy."

"You're not crazy, but remember what you promised, okay?"

"About the tiger?"

I hurried him along. "There wasn't any tiger! We proved that. I mean about getting lost the other day."

He held up one hand and stopped me before I could say anything else. "Don't fret about that. I'm not about to tell stories on myself that make me look feeble."

"Good."

He smoothed his mustache with the back of his index finger. "Spottin' that paw print, though, ain't one of those stories."

"Pappy, there wasn't any paw print!"

"Are you guys okay?" Mom asked, striding back toward us.

Pappy stared at the decorations, now just a couple of dry lawns away. "Why, look at them lanterns. I must be in China." Then he crossed his eyes and winked at me.

Mom wasn't buying it. "Don't kid around, Dad.

It's not funny." Then she glanced at me. Glanced meaningfully. And I mouthed, "He's fine."

The three of us just stood at the edge of the drive for a minute, downwind from the big barbecue pit. Walter's dad, in a tank top with a bandanna tied around his neck, tended rack after rack of ribs. I could see his tattoo twitch as he wielded a giant fork.

Then Kyle's mom—wearing jeans, a white blouse, and red rope-soled sandals—saw us, waved, and started our way. She had to skirt the microphone with its tangled wires and cross the nearly deserted driveway, where two couples were dancing to Ronnie Milsap.

Mom handed me the big salad bowl, took both of Alicia's hands, and then they kissed each other on both cheeks.

"How are you, honey?" Alicia asked, leaning toward me. She'd braided her hair, mixing red beads with little knots. It fell forward like a curtain in front of some exotic room.

Before I could answer, Pappy said to her, "Alicia, if I get the Alzheimer's tonight, just tie me to a washtub full of beer." Then he ambled away.

She smiled, showing her perfect teeth. "Sounds like a plan, Pappy."

We watched him stop in the center of the dance floor and shake hands with Mr. Wright, my teacher. Mom asked, "What am I gonna do with him?"

Mom had really been talking to herself, but Alicia said, "I miss my daddy every day. I think you're lucky just to have Pappy around."

"That's right!" I said. "Alicia's right."

"Well, help me keep an eye on him tonight, will you?"

"I already said I would."

"We all will," Alicia said. Then she looked around, sighed, and pointed to the rows of folding chairs: one group set up against the garage door, the other across the concrete drive under the HAPPY BIRTHDAY banner. All the black people—mostly relatives of Alicia's who'd come to town for her party—sat on one side, and all the white people sat on the other.

"Looks like a photograph of voter registration in the fifties, doesn't it?" Alicia said, smiling.

I followed my mom's gaze as it landed first on the folks by the garage. I could hear the low, throaty rumble of conversation, pierced every now and then by a happy shriek. Across the way, the locals sat in tight little rows like a choir. The women held cans of soda pop wrapped in napkins. The men muttered to each other, probably about gas mileage.

My mom rubbed her strong hands together. "Two, four, six, eight," she said. "I think it's time to integrate."

Alicia laughed. "Follow me. I've got a second

cousin from Oakland over here; I've been tellin' him you could dance his feet right off." And she led her away.

I was still holding the salad, so I went over and set it down on the long wooden table with its checkered cloth. I couldn't help but notice that even the food was segregated. The pineapple-marshmallow surprise regarded the candied yams suspiciously. I put the green salad down between them.

Then, half looking for my friends, half keeping track of Pappy, I wandered past Kyle's dad, who was standing by himself, looking starched and pressed in jeans and a white shirt, light glancing off his gold-rimmed glasses.

"Nice party," I said politely. "Thanks for asking us."

"You're welcome," he said in his deep god-of-thunder voice.

But he did smile when Alicia hustled up to the microphone and announced, "Folks, our favorite chiropractor is finally here, so this song's for Bonnie—'My Boyfriend's Back.' " She hammered the last word so that everybody would get the joke.

Immediately the old rock 'n' roll tune pounded out of the speakers. Mom and a tall man with a completely shaved head started to dance. They were good. I watched their feet and kept time in my head the way Mom had taught me. Or tried to teach me.

I got myself something to drink from the kids' washtub full of ice and pop. A couple of juniors (actually, they'd be seniors in September) were standing there practicing at being older: they guzzled Pepsi, tucked some Red Man tobacco in their mouths, then belched real loud, and looked around to see if any of the girls were tearing their clothes off yet because spitting tobacco juice and belching—as everybody knows—are major turn-ons.

Naturally, they acted like I wasn't even there, so I went and found my granddad, who was standing with Mr. Wright and George, one of his cronies. As I came up, Pappy threw away a long stick he'd been holding and put one arm around my waist. We stood there without saying anything, his thumb hooked onto the belt he'd bought me, our identical white straw hats bobbing, the black boots we'd polished together moving a little this way, a little that as we kept time to the music.

Then George asked, "When are you goin' to Tahoe with me, Pappy?"

"Never."

George smoothed one side of his incredible hair, as dazzlingly white as TV laundry. "I swear there's six gals to every fella, and they're lookin' for love in all the wrong places."

"Why's that? They lose their glasses?"

As Mr. Wright grinned over at me, George's eyes roamed the patio like one of those surveillance devices in a bank. "Bus leaves from the library every two weeks. We can get us a room for sixteen dollars, hang a towel on the doorknob if it's"—he paused for effect—"occupied."

I leaned in. "I'll be around, Pappy. Okay?"

"Me, too," Mr. Wright said, shaking hands. "Always a pleasure to talk to you, Pappy. Always educational."

I followed Mr. Wright. It was a little weird to see a teacher wearing shorts and huaraches. He looked like a real person. I pulled up even with him. "Can I ask you something?"

"Sure."

"It's not about school."

"Thank God."

"Well, you know my granddad. You don't think he's losin' it, do you?"

My teacher stopped and rolled his 7UP can between both palms thoughtfully. "Who says he's losing it?"

I looked around until I spotted Mom telling jokes, probably, to half a dozen grinning people.

"Ah," said Mr. Wright, putting two and two together. "Well, Jesse, people get older and they change. It happens to everybody. It'll happen to you and me."

"Sure, change. But not have to be locked up or anything."

He put his hand on my shoulder. He was strong,

and I liked it. It reminded me of how Pappy's grip used to be. And still was. Sometimes.

"My mom," he said, "went through this with her mother, who started ordering major appliances over the phone."

"What happened?"

"We sent back a lot of double-wide refrigerators."

"I mean, what happened to her? Sure, what she did was a bother and all, but it didn't really hurt anybody."

Mr. Wright drained his soda and tossed the can underhanded into a recycling box. Then he said, "She died before we had to do anything. Went to sleep and just never woke up."

"Well, Pappy's not gonna die!"

He looked at me, narrowing his eyes intently. "Jesse, you love your grandfather. Anybody can see that. And you always will. And that's good. But people change, my friend. He does. And *you* do." He held up one finger before I could interrupt. "Maybe Pappy's the exception. I hope so."

We both watched as my granddad crossed the edge of the dance floor carrying two cans of beer. Then Mr. Wright said, half to himself,

> *"Tyger! Tyger! burning bright*
> *In the forests of the night,*
> *What immortal hand or eye*
> *Could frame thy fearful symmetry?"*

Turning toward me, he asked, "Remember that?"

"It's that poem you read us." I got real suspicious real fast. "What made you think of tigers?"

"Just a little bit ago, Pappy was drawing in the dust, showing George and me the difference between tiger tracks and puma tracks."

Oh, no. "Tiger tracks? He's never seen a tiger track. Nobody around here has."

"Well, he had me convinced. Anyway, that's when I thought about the Blake poem: Pappy's still burning pretty bright, if you ask me."

Just then Walter appeared. He was like Tinker Bell, darting everywhere.

"We're all in the kitchen, Jesse. C'mon." He grinned up at Mr. Wright. "Thanks for the C-plus. Paul says thanks, too." Then he glanced up at me. "Jesse helped me a lot. He read my first draft and told me to change some stuff. But I wrote it all," he insisted. .

"I know that. I'd recognize your unique style any-where." As they shook hands, he added, "You should keep a journal, Walter. You've got a million-dollar imagination."

"Did I tell you about candy pajamas? They're so when you wake up hungry at night you could just eat your sleeve."

Mr. Wright looked down at his huaraches and laughed. "I promised Ms. Ortega a dance. See you guys later, okay?"

We all turned to look at Marisol Ortega. She was wearing the tallest shoes I'd ever seen, and huge red stick-on nails that made it look like her fingers were wearing stilts, too.

I was following Walter toward the kitchen when I ran into my mom.

"I'm just gonna sit with Dad awhile," she said.

Oh, jeez. I looked over at Pappy, who was pointing down at the dust again. The last thing I wanted was for her to see him drawing tiger tracks.

"Let's dance instead," I blurted, shaking my fingers like I was about to shoot the game-winning free throw.

Her face brightened. "Really?"

"Sure, I'll lead."

I took a big breath, as if I were about to jump off the high dive, then put my left hand in hers and the other one on her red-and-white beaded belt. Counting quietly to myself, I waited for a good place in Willie Nelson's "Always on My Mind," and started in.

Mom was grinning at me. "You're doing fine."

"You're helping me turn. I usually just dance right into the wall."

Mom pressed down on me like I was a brake pedal. "If we hit a wall at this speed, we're both going to get whiplash."

"Sorry. I guess it makes me nervous, dancing with my mother."

"Why is that, Dr. Freud?"

That made me giggle, which made me wish I'd at least managed a deep chuckle. Mom just grinned her crooked, smart-aleck grin, which I'd inherited, and patted me on the shoulder. Then I felt her hand start creeping toward the center of my back.

"You're out a little," she said. "Right up here by this first dorsal verta—"

"Will you stop feeling my spine when there's people around!"

"All right. All right. We'll talk about something else. How's Dad?"

"He's fine."

"That's like saying, 'He's not on fire yet.' "

"Mr. Wright said he was fine."

"Oh, well—then it must be true."

"Look, Mom, let's talk about something else."

"We just talked about something else."

"Did you like dancing with that cousin of Alicia's?"

She brightened. "Did I ever! When I put my arm around him, I thought, Oh, baby. He had vertebrae to die for."

"Why don't you go out with Vic again? I saw you dancing with him, too, and you looked pretty good together."

Mom made a face. "Vic wears a lift in his left shoe. His sacroiliac goes out if he sneezes. I'm sorry, but I have very high spinal standards."

As the song ended and we both clapped politely, I looked at my glistening palm.

"What do I tell a girl if I sweat like this?"

"Tell her you're nervous."

I frowned. "That's not too cool."

"Well, it's the truth. And she's gonna be nervous, too, so she'll probably like you for being honest."

Over her shoulder I saw Kyle through the kitchen window, so I told Mom I was going inside.

"Okay, I'll keep an eye on Pappy."

"C'mon. He's not some kid who needs to be watched all the time. Leave him alone."

"Honey, wake up and smell the beans. Sometimes he's more of a kid than you are."

"But—" Just then Alicia came toward us with another cousin in tow, and I breathed a sigh of relief. "You dance," I said. "Pappy's fine." We looked at him, some twenty yards away.

"What's he doing with that stick?" Mom asked.

"Um, you know, showing Mr. Wright how things used to be around here. You know, where stuff was and all."

"But he's not talking to Mr. Wright."

"Mom! What do you think he's doing—pointing out all the places he's gonna burn down later on?"

She sighed. "Maybe you're right. Maybe I should just dance."

On my way to the house, I got trapped behind two locals. They had their cowboy hats pulled low, and the curved brims—curled almost to a point in front—pecked at each other.

"It's the damn politicians that did it."

"Not the Republicans' fault it didn't rain."

"Ain't just the rain. It's what's been done to the land in the meantime."

"I still say they should've floated them desaliniza-tion bonds."

Stuck, I backtracked and slid past two kids a few years older than I was. Each wore a Walkman and what looked like pajamas from Jamaica.

A flashbulb going off made me turn around. Ni-gel's folks had arrived. Thomas, dangling cameras and equipment, was already snapping pictures. Mau-reen—sporting a long, embroidered peasant skirt and forty pounds of silver jewelry—headed straight for Alicia. I heard her ask, "What can I do to help?"

Nigel glided up beside me. "Apparently my mother assumed this was a fiesta. If she'd known so many black people were going to be here, she'd have worn her dashiki."

I told him I thought the guys were in the kitchen.

"I'll bet Paul is."

I took one more look at Pappy before I went in-side, where Walter and Kyle were gulping cans of Dr Pepper and talking while Paul peered into the refrigerator. He was wearing white overalls over a white T-shirt; a white straw hat perched on his big head. He looked like a farmer who grew snow.

Nigel took in the hunting knife strapped to Walter's waist. "What's that for?"

Walter patted the chipped handle. "That tiger Pappy saw could be anywhere."

"There's no tiger!" I said. "Will you just stop with the tiger?"

"Anyway," Nigel pointed out, "Jesse's grandfather said to be considerate of animals, not stab them."

"Hey, this isn't to stab the tiger. It's to stab the guy who'd try and hurt the tiger."

"What guy?"

"The guy who brought him over here. You don't think he came on his own, do you?"

Before Nigel could ask, "What guy?" again, Paul turned to Kyle. "Why's your dad got pictures of cows all over the house?"

Even in the kitchen, there were framed photographs of Brangus, all with the cattle standing sideways.

"How can you tell 'em apart?" Paul asked, brandishing a brick of Velveeta like a candy bar.

Kyle shrugged. "I can't all the time, but Dad can. They're pretty much individuals to him."

Paul leaned to inspect one. "Growin' cows sounds easy. Don't you kind of match 'em up and just stand back?"

"It's not that crude," Kyle said. "They talk on the phone first, then go out for alfalfa."

I laughed and let him take my can of soda and finish it. Then he ran one hand over his new haircut; it was the same on top, but the sides had been tapered and shaved, and it gave him a speedy look.

As he pushed the flowered curtains aside and peered out at the barbecue pit, I asked, "Can you see Pappy? He's not talking to my mom, is he?"

"Uh-uh. He's talkin' to Nigel's dad."

"Good. Has he got a stick in his hand or is he drawing in the dust with something?"

"Nope."

"Even better."

Walter hauled himself up onto the tall counter like he was climbing out of a swimming pool. "There's Kathy Johnson. She sits behind me in math." Then he lowered himself to the floor again and wiped both hands on his jeans, which were so long the bottoms were frayed where he'd walked on them. "Girls make me nervous," he admitted. "I have to pee when I'm around girls."

"They don't want to know that," Nigel advised.

Outside, Kyle's dad stepped up to the microphone and tapped for silence, so we all filed out the side door.

"Folks," he said, sounding both solemn and nervous, "just before we eat, I want to say I'm glad you all could come." He pointed to the HAPPY BIRTHDAY sign. "It's been a tough year, but it doesn't show on

Alicia, does it? She's just as pretty as the happy day she agreed to be my wife."

He took a big breath, waving down the smattering of applause. Then he announced, with more gusto, "Bobby Bonita's gonna play for us while you line up for barbecue. So thanks again for comin', and have a good time."

I watched some locals, their empty plates held out like panhandlers, detour way around the dancers.

Kyle materialized at my side as Paul started to snap his fingers and rock back and forth.

"Do you feel something," Kyle asked, "that should register about five-point-two on the Richter scale, or is Paul dancing?"

"Go, big guy!" I yelled, as Paul, both arms straight out, shimmied toward the center of the dance floor.

As my mom bopped past she yelled, "So that's The Airplane dance you were talking about!"

I just nodded, fascinated. Paul was good.

A couple of Kyle's cousins pranced out to meet him. He'd raise his arms; they'd raise their arms. He'd shake his booty; they'd shake their booties. He'd swoop around like a stealth bomber; they'd swoop around. A bunch of other people joined in, keeping their eyes on Paul and the two girls, doing what they did.

Everybody got a kick out of it. People were laughing and clapping and grinning and giving each other big helpings of everything on the table.

When the song ended, Paul—dripping like a fire fighter—staggered back toward us. We pumped his big damp hand and slapped him on the back.

"You were great!" Walter cried. "I didn't know you could do that."

Paul's face was as red as a calendar sunset. "I got carried away. I usually just dance at home. By myself. You know?"

"You can dance, my friend," said Kyle.

Paul blotted his forehead with a handful of napkins. "Really?"

"My cousins don't boogie with just anybody."

"I better eat," Paul said. "I think I'm gonna faint."

We were piling our plates full, and I mean full, when Nigel's dad stepped up beside me. The sleeves of his khaki shirt were rolled halfway up, and I could see two silver bracelets.

"I was talking to your grandfather," he said with a smile. Then he patted one of his cameras. "Got some great pictures. Could have listened to him forever. He's a wonderful storyteller. A living archive."

"Tell my mom."

He reached for some salad. "Why is that?"

"Aw, forget it. He is great, isn't he?"

Thomas nodded. "A national treasure." Then he took a quick picture and strolled away.

A minute later we carried our plates over to where

the others had settled. As we sat down, Paul leaned over a mound of barbecue so tall it got all over the bib of his overalls.

"Those black guys," he whispered, "are really checking us out." He shifted his eyes toward the two brothers in the elaborate pajamas. "If they come over here, is there like any black thing we ought to know?"

Kyle picked up a piece of corn bread. He glanced over at me, and I could almost see his mind work.

"Actually," he said, "yeah, there is. They belong to a gang called the Ebony Wolves."

Paul flinched. "Jeez, they sound bad."

Kyle shook his head. "Not if you know their sign."

"Cool," said Walter. "What is it?"

Kyle pushed his plate to one side and leaned in. "I don't want everybody to see this," he whispered. Then he held his hand out, like he was going to karate-chop something. Up came the thumb, then he bent his index finger in.

I started to shovel potato salad into my mouth so that I wouldn't start laughing. When we were little and we'd made shadow animals, this was how we did the dog.

Paul, wide-eyed, was fixing his right hand with his left. Then he leaned over and helped Walter, and they both showed Kyle.

He adjusted their thumbs solemnly. "So when these guys come over, just be cool until it's time to throw 'em their sign, and don't forget to howl."

Walter looked at Paul. Paul looked at Walter. They both looked at Kyle. "Howl?"

"Like a wolf. Like an ebony wolf."

"Oh, yeah. Got it."

Right on cue the two guys sauntered over and stood by Kyle. When one held out his hand, Kyle took it and they performed some intricate ritual.

"Our folks," said the kid with a lift-off haircut, "told us to make sure to say thanks and all." He pointed to a tall woman in white pants tucked into shiny red boots. "Our mom married your mom's cousin, or somethin' like that."

Kyle nodded. "You're from South Central, right? Name's Rashad?"

"Tell it," said the tall one, who wore a miniature Africa around his neck on a thong. Then he looked the table over. "These your homeboys?"

"Yeah."

"You Jesse?" he asked, looking at me.

"Uh-huh."

He glanced behind him. "Some pretty mama named Heather likes you, man."

"God, now it's in L.A."

Kyle pointed to everyone else in turn—"Gargantua, Viper, Thunderbolt."

Nigel touched his lips with the edge of a napkin. "Thunderbolt?" he said wryly.

Rashad looked the table over. "Well, we're—"

"We know," boomed Paul. He and Walter stuck their hands out, made their thumbs waggle and their little fingers bark. They threw back their heads and howled: "Ahh-wooo. Ahh-wooo. Ah-wooo, woo, woo!"

Rashad and his friend froze, then backed up a step or two. "We, uh, gotta jam now," he finally choked out. "Catch you later."

"Bye, bro!" cried Walter as they turned away. Then he leaned toward Kyle. "How'd we do?"

"You impressed 'em," Kyle assured him.

While the rest of us ate, Paul just looked down at his plate. Finally he said, "I think I'm gonna take some of this back."

Kyle stared at him. "Why?"

"Well, maybe I was thinkin' I could dance better if I was, you know, a little lighter on my feet."

"Take it home," I suggested. "For later."

"All right. Cool. My folks couldn't come, so . . . yeah, I'll take it home." He turned to Kyle. "Can I go get some foil and stuff from your kitchen?"

"I'll go, too," cried Walter, before Kyle could even answer. "Then you can show me some of those steps."

Just as they left, Pappy wandered up and plopped

down in an empty chair across from us. He pointed to the three-piece band and half translated the moody Spanish song. "Somebody's in love," Pappy mused, "and somebody else's heart is broken."

I indulged him. "Thanks, we were wondering."

"I worked with a fella from Mexico once," Pappy said over the accordion of Bobby Bonita and the Barn Burners, "who hated Roy Rogers. Said he saw a movie once and Roy knocked down a bunch of Mexican cowboys with one punch. I forget that old boy's name."

"Francisco Mena." Kyle and I said it in unison.

Pappy sat up straight, looking amazed. "How'd you know that?"

"You told us this story about a hundred times," Kyle pointed out.

"Was this before or after I lost my mind?"

I rolled my eyes. "You haven't lost your mind."

We looked up as headlights swept across the garage wall, the dance floor, the towering pepper tree. A red GMC Sierra pulled right up, almost touching a deserted table.

Bobby Yates had no more than got out and hurried around to help his dad when kids started to make bogus ostrich sounds. They came from everywhere: behind someone's hand, hidden by a hat brim— gravelly big-bird caws that somebody'd made up the day of the ostrich races.

As the out-of-towners looked around warily,

Bobby put his hands on his hips and glared. In his bolo tie and boot-cut jeans, he looked like a square dancer with an attitude.

"Very funny," he said. "I'm laughin' so hard I might hurt myself."

Bobby's dad, who was dressed in a pale-blue suit that had fit him once but now looked like somebody else's, peered around until he found my granddad.

Pappy watched Mr. Yates use his right arm to move his left one. Then he drained his can of beer and got up. "Some choice," he muttered. "You either have a stroke or forget which end of your horse to feed."

As the stereo came on again, Kyle glanced at the band, which was packing up.

"Want to dance?"

"Together, you mean? What's your dad going to think?"

Kyle threw a handful of clean napkins at me. "I thought you'd want to actually talk to Heather."

"Maybe you better talk to her and tell me what she says. I'm used to that."

"Maybe I should just dance with her and tell you how she feels."

We looked until we found Heather Hughes. In her new leather mini. Just then she stood up, tugged at her skirt, then sat down again.

"God," I said. "She's way taller than me all of a sudden."

"You're the same height; just her hair is taller than yours."

"Maybe I'll let my hair ask her hair to dance, and I'll watch from here."

"C'mon."

Alone on the dance floor, I took a deep breath. Heather was sitting between two girlfriends, who scanned the party suspiciously. When one of them spotted me, she leaned into Heather and whispered. Immediately all six eyes swung my way. And focused. I felt like something in a petri dish.

Heart beating fast, I put my head down, leaned forward, and let the laws of physics—bodies in motion—carry me to their table. On the way I practiced: "Heather, would you like to dance? Heather, would you like to dance? Heather, would you like to dance?"

"Weather, could you hike . . ." Thank God I got stuck. But then nothing at all would come out. I reached up and felt my throat.

While Heather just stared, her two friends leaned forward. They nodded encouragement. I watched them mime the words. One hugged herself.

"Like?" I guessed.

She nodded and clapped silently. The other one held her left hand up, put her right one on her tummy, and swayed dreamily.

"Dance?"

Nodding, they each held up two fingers.

"*To* dance?"

"Good, Jesse," one hissed. "Now put it together."

"Uh, would you like to dance?"

They pointed at their leader.

"Oh, yeah. Heather, would you like to dance?"

Then we all stared at Heather, who was thoughtfully sipping a Coke.

"All right," she said after what seemed like a decade.

The other girls slumped into their chairs, exhausted.

"But these shoes just came in the mail." I watched her hair ascend. "They're the only ones in town. They're unique."

I looked down. "I won't step on them." I glanced at the other two just to make sure I'd said something rational, and they nodded.

But Heather just stood there like a tree. I could have tied a hammock to her.

"Do you know how to do this?" she demanded.

"I thought so, but . . ."

"Don't put your arm all the way around me. It's too hot."

I let my right hand rest on her waist. The feel of the leather made me smile.

"What are you thinking about?" Heather demanded.

"Oh," I blurted, "just that you might be wearing one of Kyle's dad's cows."

She made a face. "I thought you weren't a total jerk."

"You asked me what I was think—"

"Are we dancing or standing still? Everyone's staring at us."

I slid flat-footed a few inches. Then I just rocked her back and forth. Heather looked like a metronome, ticktocking.

When I felt my hand begin to perspire, I remembered what my mom had said. "I'm a little nervous," I confessed. "That's why I'm sweating."

"Yuck!" Heather snatched her hand away and waved it around.

Just then the song ended. Kyle was standing nearby.

"Let's switch!" Heather announced.

"But I thought you liked me," I blurted.

She looked like I'd just told her I kept Jell-O in my hat. "What in the world ever gave you that idea?" Then she pulled Kyle's cousin away from him, and planted her in front of me.

"Dance with Kinisha," she said.

"You don't have to," I said to Kinisha.

"It's okay." She had a nice smile.

As Kyle and Heather disappeared into the crowd of dancers, I wiped my palms on my jeans. "Heather had new shoes," I explained.

"Big ones," Kinisha said, and I laughed.

Her hand was warm and even a little damp, but

not in any gross way. I wanted to talk, but couldn't think of a single thing to say. My mind felt as empty and swirly as a chalkboard.

I finally blurted, "I like your name."

"It's African. My mom's really into the whole African thing."

"Well, I like it."

"I guess." She tugged at one of the thin straps on her yellow tank top. "But I've never been to Africa and I don't much want to go. Are you named after a cowboy?"

"Jesse James, I guess." I could talk to Kinisha and dance, too. She moved with me easily. "The great American crook."

Kinisha smiled. "You look pretty honest to me, Jesse."

"How'd you know my name? Did Kyle tell you?"

"No. Your grandfather did. We were talking, and he said you were a great dancer."

"Oh, man." I groaned. "Now you think my grandfather has to fix me up."

Kinisha grinned and danced a little closer. "He was telling me about—"

"I know—tigers. He kind of exaggerates sometimes."

She nodded, and as she did, her sweet-smelling hair brushed my cheek. "My grandma Bessie did that."

"Did she live with you guys?"

111

Just then Bobby Yates lost his balance and toppled over backward. Like a true drunk, he held on to his can of beer and didn't spill a drop.

"I tripped," he said, grabbing at the nearest table, which immediately fell over. A plate of ribs went flying, then landed on him, making mysterious hieroglyphics on his white shirt.

Kinisha looked at me. "My mom'll want to go home now," she said with a grin. "She always splits right after the first person passes out."

"But Bobby Yates always passes out. It doesn't mean anything."

She smiled. "It's late, anyway. Maybe I'll see you again sometime."

I watched her walk away. She was very thin and her jeans were huge, folded over at the waist a couple of times to make a kind of fat sash. But that didn't mean they didn't look good on her, because they did.

When Kyle passed her, she held out one hand and he brushed it lightly. Then he came and stood by me.

"Did Heather tell you about her new shoes?" I asked.

He shook his head. "She just talked about you."

"But when we were dancing, all she did was get on my case."

"Maybe she likes you from a distance."

"Maybe we should be pen pals."

All around us, people packed up their things and wandered away, waving and calling back from the darkness.

"Pretty good party," Kyle said. "Ate a lot, danced a little."

"Messed with Paul's mind."

"And Walter's. Don't forget Walter."

Then I spotted my mom, who was all of a sudden bearing down on me. I felt like a little rowboat bobbing in front of a big white steamer. I didn't mean to, but I took a step backward.

"What's all this nonsense," she said in a hoarse whisper, "about there being a tiger up in the foothills?"

I pointed to Kyle. "C'mon, Mom."

She glanced at him and frowned. "So?"

"So can we argue in private? This is embarrassing," I whispered.

She looked puzzled. "Kyle's family. And who's arguing? I'm asking if you know anything about what my dad told Old Man Yates, which is that there's a tiger roaming the Santa Rios."

"God, Mom. He was probably just tryin' to give Mr. Yates a little rush. I mean, look at him."

The three of us turned to look at Bobby's dad, who sat holding his left arm in his lap and staring into space.

"How did all this start?" Mom asked, but a little quieter.

113

"When Pappy and I were up in the hills, we saw some mountain lion tracks, but that's no big deal. We almost always see mountain lion tracks."

"You both saw them?"

"Sure," I lied.

"Then why is he tellin' everybody he saw tiger tracks?"

I grabbed her arm. "So? He's just tellin', you know, tall tales." I glared at her. "Why do you always think the worst about your own dad?"

Kyle stepped between us. "Hey, hey," he said. "No fighting. It's still a party, okay?"

Mom narrowed her eyes more, like she was trying to see inside me, and asked, "You're not coverin' up for him, are you, Jesse?"

"No," I lied.

She sighed, then grabbed me hard and kissed me on the cheek. Then she reached for Kyle and kissed him explosively, too. We both just stood there, half-stunned, while she walked away.

Finally Kyle pawed at his damp cheek as he turned to me. "What happens when Pappy really screws up?"

"He won't."

"Well, I hope not, 'cause you're weavin' some seriously tangled webs, bro."

"Maybe." I looked for my granddad and saw him sitting alone, staring down at a silver can of Coors Light. "But it's worth it."

I sat straight up in bed. The smell of smoke was strong in the morning air. "Oh, man," I said out loud. "He's done it now!"

Sure enough, by the time I'd tugged on a pair of jeans, grabbed my hat, and bolted into the living room, the smoke was blanket-thick and gray-green as smog. I heard the bouncy organ music, but could barely make out the TV, where Dorothy Hamill sped across the ice.

"Pappy!" I shook my grandfather, then grabbed both his cold hands and tugged. Even while I did, I could see what'd happened: Pappy's cigarette had missed the washtub of sand, and the fire had followed a paper trail right over to the couch.

Why didn't I pick up that sports section? I thought as long arms of flame lashed out, then broke away from the green upholstery. Red fingers arced for the beamed ceiling and for the drapes, which were already stirring eerily.

"Granddad! Come on!" I got him to his feet as both his eyes flew open. He looked around, put two and two together, then swore and, coughing, bolted for the kitchen with my arm around his waist.

As the two of us stood bent over, sputtering and hacking, Mom came charging between us with a garden hose.

"Call nine-one-one!" she bellowed, pushing me toward the phone on the wall.

I watched Pappy stumble out the back door and into the yard. Then I punched the buttons—getting it wrong the first time—and yelled, "Fire!" at the operator, my eyes fixed on my mother.

I rushed halfway into the living room, but she was doing fine on her own. She looked almost funny with her pink quilted housecoat, roper's boots, and toilet paper wrapped around a new hairdo.

"Get out!" she shouted over one shoulder.

"But it's just about over, Mom. Everything's gonna be okay!"

Both legs had been burned off one end of the couch, so it slumped like a foundered steer.

"Get out, anyway." She jerked the hose hard and moved farther into the room. "Go flag down the fire truck."

When I heard the sirens a few minutes later, Mom rushed outside, too, while the guys in their yellow slickers piled off the lime-green engine and charged in.

Mrs. Johnson's Coccyx, quacking wildly, scurried among the tall black boots. "Will somebody get that duck!"

Most of the fire fighters carried big, red, podlike fire extinguishers, and I could hear the powerful *pffffsst, pffffsst* as they prowled the living room. I watched a neighbor lady put one hand on Mom's shoulder, take the bobby pins out of the toilet paper, and fluff at her blond hair.

Just about everybody who drove by stopped, so the pickups and old dusty cars were starting to clot up in the dry grass along the side of the road, and I had to sift through the nosy neighbors to get to Pappy. He was leaning on the fence, his back to the house. Our horses, Cody and Marky Mark, had bolted to the farthest corner of the lot.

I watched my grandfather lean and put his forehead against the smooth wood the two of us had notched and hammered into a corral. When Pappy didn't wear a hat or pull his long hair back, it looked pretty thin. I could see right down to the scalp, which was awfully white-looking.

When I slipped in next to him, Pappy coughed and cleared his throat. Then he rasped, "Your mother's right about me."

"It was just an accident!" I tugged at the bony shoulder. "C'mon."

Pappy shook his head as he put one hand to his chest and rubbed. "Give me a minute alone now, son."

I half turned away, spotting my mom and, right beside her with a casserole dish, Mrs. Ezlock, who had a ninety-band citizen's radio from Radio Shack; her tuna surprise was famous for beating the fire engine to the tragedy. I'd laughed at her before; now it gave me the creeps.

Pretty soon the fire fighters came out and said that everything was okay and could have been a lot worse.

"Jesse woke up first," Mom said, "and got Pappy out."

"Good for you." Barney from the feed-and-grain store patted me clumsily with his huge glove. Just then the radio at his belt crackled and somebody from the truck yelled. "Must be a full moon," he said, taking one last critical look at the house.

As Mom and I—and just about everybody else—drifted toward the side door, she looked toward Pappy and asked me, "Is he all right?"

"I think so." But when I hesitated, she tugged at me.

"I need you in here, and he needs to think about this by himself."

"TV's shot," said someone from the living room as the men began toting out the big stuff and the women wove themselves among them, touching

118

something to make sure it wasn't hot, lifting some-thing else with the toe of one boot or shoe, then letting it drop back onto the soggy floor.

Mom stood in the kitchen, her back to the hubbub, phone to one ear, index finger in the other. I heard her say, "I just wanted to check. We've been on that list forever."

"You know, Jesse," said Mrs. Ezlock, lifting up the drapes and sniffing them, "this isn't half bad. Why, Sunu and I had a fire once when we was livin' up by Abel."

I stared at the scorched carpet. It looked like a flying saucer had landed on it.

"Are you listenin', Jesse? One second we're sittin' on the porch drinkin' Tang, and the next there ain't nothin' but a hole in the ground the dogs wouldn't go near."

"Gangway!" A quartet of cowboys, one on each corner, lifted the dripping couch and carried it out-side.

Mrs. Ezlock leaned to pick up a half-burned copy of *Prevention* magazine. "You all are lucky, Jesse."

With what was left of the drapes torn down, I could see Pappy slumped against the corral. "Yes, ma'am," I said automatically. "I guess we are."

Behind me, I heard my mom ask, "How much a month? Is that a new figure?"

"Bonnie?" A neighbor wearing a denim jacket with no shirt underneath yelled for my mom.

"She's busy."

He tested the floor where the couch had been. "This isn't even gonna have to be replaced." He looked toward the kitchen. "Bonnie!"

Her hand emerged, but it was hard to tell whether that meant "Okay" or "Go away." I heard her shout, "Then give me *their* number. You act like Osco's on the other side of the world."

Half a minute later she slammed the phone down and stormed into the living room. "What needs to be done here?" she demanded.

The other people stared at each other. Then one of the men ventured, "Not a lot, Bonnie. Just carry a little more of this stuff on outside, then mop it up and sweep it out, I guess."

She put her hands on her hips. "Well, just let me climb into some pants, and we'll get it done."

It took quite a while. I worked, too, glancing out the window regularly at Pappy, who'd turned around and hunkered down, his back to a cedar post. The gander stood beside him.

The yard was full of people who'd stopped off, so by the time Mom'd thanked everyone, hugged most of them, and waved the rest good-bye, it was getting toward noon. Pappy was all by himself.

I went out through the propped-open side door, took off my hat, and put it on my grandfather as Mom marched right up beside us.

"I could have lost you both," she said through

120

clenched teeth. "And *you*"—she looked down at her father—"you could have killed Jesse."

"Mom!"

Pappy put a restraining hand on my arm. "She's right, boy. I'm the worst kind of old man. Useless and a hazard to boot."

"It was an accident." I looked frantically from one adult to the other. "It could have happened to anybody."

Pappy shook his head. "It didn't, though. It happened to me."

"That's right," Mom said before she turned and strode away.

I patted my grandfather clumsily. "We all feel bad now. It'll be better tomorrow, and then pretty soon we'll forget it. Okay?" I shook him gently.

Pappy put a hand out and I helped him up. The old man rubbed the back of his neck with one hand. "Heck of a note, ain't it. I've took care of things all my life: all kinds of animals, your mom when she was little, your grandma when she took sick, then you. And now I can't take care of myself."

"Sure you can. You just need a little help sometimes, that's all." I looked toward my mother's office, then guided my grandfather toward the house. "C'mon and lie down for a little while. You'll feel better later on."

Pappy dug out his sack of tobacco and flat package of Zig Zag rolling papers. "Take these. I'm never gonna smoke again unless maybe it's in the middle of the road where a truck can hit me."

I took the soft makings. "I'll just hold 'em for you. Now, c'mon. Let's go on inside, and you can rest."

Minutes later, I pulled my granddad's boots off and watched him stretch out and almost instantly fall asleep. Then I hurried through the living room— wet, burned out, scorched—down the gravel drive, through the waiting room, and right up to the door of my mother's apartment. I knocked hard and was told to come in.

Automatically I stepped out of my boots, then crossed the sand-colored carpet toward the half-open door to the bedroom.

"Pappy's asleep," I announced, leaning on the wall without looking in.

"Good."

I heard a drawer slide open and shut. Then the hangers in the closet rattled. "Are you goin' somewhere special?" I asked suspiciously.

"Osco."

"What for?"

"Pappy."

"Is somebody charging you by the word? I need a little longer answer here, Mom."

My mother stepped into the living room, fussing with a blue scarf. Otherwise she had on a white blouse I'd never seen before and pressed jeans. New ones.

"It must be a hundred out," I exclaimed. "You're gonna burn up worse than the living room."

"I am trying to look presentable."

"What are you doin', Mom?" I demanded.

"I'm going to Golden Shadows. It's that new nursing home in Osco."

"Osco's right next door to a nuclear-waste dump!"

She shook her head vigorously. "*Might* be next door to a nuclear-waste site. Possibly. In the future. But we're talking about right now. Today. Pappy's goin' somewhere he can't hurt anybody, including himself. There's no room at Golden Oaks right now, so if this—"

"I heard you. The place was still smoking and you were already on the phone trying to get rid of—"

Mom pumped up the volume. "So if this Golden Shadows place is clean and safe, I'm taking the money out of the savings and he's in there. And I mean tomorrow."

"Mom!" I pleaded. "You can't!"

"No? You watch me. Most of my life Pappy was there for me when I needed him. It didn't matter if he wanted to or not—he did what he thought was best. Well, now I'm doing what I think is best for him." She pointed to herself and then at me. "And for us, too."

I waved both arms. "Are you nuts? He fed you

and bought you clothes, then took care of me and helped put you through chiropractor's school."

Mom looked at herself in the mirror, tugging hard at the blue scarf. "My mother died just about the time you were born. You and I put some life back into that old Bouquet Canyon house."

"You *had* to come home. When Dad just split like that, you were all alone and you had me."

Mom shook her head. "No, sir! I had friends all over San Francisco. I did what had to be done by coming back to Norbu. He needed me then 'cause he was grieving; he needs me now to decide for him."

I looked for my mom's eyes in the mirror. "Hasn't he got a say in this?"

She turned and pointed toward the main house. "That burned-out front room up there is a pretty powerful say, if you ask me."

"How can you treat him like this? He gave you the money to buy this house. Why can't he burn part of it if he wants to? It's his."

She shook her head so hard that her hairdo almost moved. "No, no, no. He left me the money before he died is all. That's exactly what he said when he sold the ranch and signed the check over to me: that there was no reason to wait."

"So now you're kicking him out."

Mom snorted. "I don't think fifteen hundred dollars a month to anyplace Golden is exactly kicking anybody out."

"But he doesn't want to go!"

She whirled around, facing me. "Well, I didn't want to get up at five in the morning and milk cows, either. I didn't want to help him butcher and plow, and I sure didn't plan to open my practice in this godforsaken town, but that's the way things worked out for me then. And this"—she pointed again toward the still-smoking room—"is the way things worked out for him now."

I glared right back. "You sound like you're getting back at him. You almost sound glad."

She looked down at her black boots, the ones with the little chains around the heels, and kicked hard at the soft nap of the carpet. When she finally did say something, her voice was much softer. "Jesse, here's what you don't understand: It's gonna get worse. Maybe little by little, maybe real fast. Either way, I just can't sit around and do nothin' while he burns himself up and you, too."

"At least," I pleaded, "think about it. Wait till he wakes up. Talk it over with him."

She glanced around the room, then seized her purse, the straw one with the jewel-eyed poodle on the side.

"I'm goin' now," she said. "You stay with Pappy."

I gritted my teeth. "He doesn't need a baby-sitter."

"Oh, no? What about—"

"This morning was an accident."

When she started for the door, I lunged in front of her. "I'm going, too!"

Mom sighed. I could almost hear her counting to ten. "We'll stop next door," she said evenly, "and ask Mrs. Waymon to keep an eye on things."

I slept all the way to Osco, and when the car finally stopped, I didn't exactly know where I was or why I was in the station wagon with my head on my mom's leg and her hand on my shoulder, just like when I was little.

I sat up, blinking and rubbing my eyes. I'd been sweating and my cheek felt wrinkled and damp as an old washrag.

"You okay?" my mom asked. "You slept hard."

"Are we there?"

"Afraid so."

I stared out at the low peach-colored building and took in the curving ramp and the wide doors. I read the sign, GOLDEN SHADOWS, with a big silhouette of a giant tree at each end, shading the G and the S.

I pushed my hair back. "If everything's so golden

when you get old, why do people end up living in places like this?"

Mom sounded matter-of-fact. "I think the myth is they're *supposed* to be golden years."

"This place is creepy." I leaned on the dashboard for a second, then jerked my arm back and rubbed the heat away.

"You can't tell a care facility by its cover," Mom said, obviously trying to lighten things up. "But it sure doesn't look as nice as Golden Oaks."

"That was creepy, too," I muttered.

She regarded me skeptically. "How would you know? You stayed outside and played."

She spit out the last word as though I'd done something terrible, like sell drugs to kittens.

"I was barely twelve."

Mom tugged at her blouse where it was stuck to her side. "Oh, big deal."

"Well, a year means a lot when you're a kid. It's not like for you."

She opened her door and the heat poured in. "Oh, fine. Now I'm old." She looked at her hair in the rearview mirror, then tried to smile. "Maybe you should go back to sleep. We got along fine on the ride up here."

Inside, as Mom talked to a receptionist, I hung back and looked the place over. To my right was a big room with round tables, hard-looking sofas, and two TVs. On the light-green walls somebody had hung watercolors. They'd been ripped right out of a big pad, because the jagged holes showed at the top. Like the kids' murals in Norbu, these were all about rain—there were big blue drops falling on giant red flowers, huge black thunderstorms with Zeus-sized bolts flying out of them, and stick people in black bathing suits diving into rippling pools.

". . . and this is my son. Jesse, this is Mrs. Mellon."

I looked up at a lady in a pantsuit the same lime-green color as Norbu's fire engine. Her glasses dangled from a silver chain around her neck and they swung back and forth as she leaned down. When she tried to smooth my hair, I stepped away.

"This kind of thing upsets them," Mrs. Mellon said to Mom.

"I'm not a *them*," I snapped.

Mrs. Mellon led us down the hall. She talked loud and she gestured a lot with her hands. She reminded me of someone on the Home Shopping Club channel.

She knew everybody's name and made a point of announcing it whenever she peeked into a room or passed someone moving slowly up or down the hall.

"Jesse?"

I'd been watching a man in Jolly Green Giant pants and white shoes who slowly twirled a golf club like a lazy drum major.

"Jesse? Come and look at this room."

I glanced in dutifully. There were two beds with a green curtain bunched between them. A narrow window looked out onto a dead acacia tree.

"They learn to share the TV," Mrs. Mellon said, pointing to a small Sony attached to the wall.

"Pappy doesn't like to share," I informed her, "and he only watches ice-skating."

"Is he a former athlete?" Mrs. Mellon asked politely.

I shook my head. "He just likes the part where the girls skate backward and their little skirts blow up over their butts."

"I don't suppose," Mom asked, "you have an adjacent facility for the terminally sassy?"

Mrs. Mellon smiled like she'd had a big slice of pickle pizza. "Let me show you the recreation area."

When the wide door at the west end of the building opened on its own, the heat stopped all three of us for a second. Mrs. Mellon's hand flew to the top button of her suit and she twisted it like a dial.

She pointed to more than a dozen men and women gathered around a long putting green made of artificial turf. "Their circulation is poor," she explained, "so they like the heat."

Everybody was dressed in colors sharp enough to make me want to reach for my sunglasses: sun yellow, igloo white, a red like cartoon flames, and jewel blue. The old men wore baseball caps with crossed golf clubs above the visors. They prowled the narrow green while half a dozen women sat nearby.

Mom pointed to the round, white tables, which held tall glasses, some topped by colorful umbrellas. "Pappy would like this part," she said.

Mrs. Mellon assured her they weren't real drinks. "Just virgin Marys, Shirley Temples, and plain iced tea."

"He couldn't even have a beer in this place," I muttered.

A minute or so later my mom and Mrs. Mellon sat in one corner of the air-conditioned rec room and talked. I slumped in a nearby chair and tried to imagine Pappy watching the news that didn't have anything to do with him, reading magazines about other people. No horse, no Dorothy Hamill tapes, no cronies. And no me.

I tuned back in as my mom was saying, ". . . a licensed chiropractor. I'd come to see Dad, anyway, so I thought if someone needed an adjustment, maybe we could barter."

Mrs. Mellon said, "I'm sorry, dear, but it wouldn't work. Our prices are fixed. And, anyway, say you treat someone on Friday, and on Saturday she's feeling poorly. Maybe she tells a guilty son or daughter, and the next thing we know, we've got a lawsuit on our hands."

Mom pushed back her bangs, brand-new this

week. "I know a little about guilt myself." Then she shrugged and stood up.

We drove through Osco, which looked like it had been built overnight by angry elves interested only in fast food and cars: McDonald's, Arby's, Trak Auto, Western Auto, Jiffy Lube, Hose Itz, Sizzler.

From my window, I eyed a gang of kids on skateboards who kept pace with our Subaru. They were grimy and scabby. And they all sported a kind of hat that looked like a dirty angel food cake with a brim. One wore a cut-off sweatshirt with OSCO LIONS across the front of it, and he had his jeans on inside out. I wondered if these same kids would be the ones who'd cruise down to Norbu on Fridays for the homicidal high school football games. Would Pappy be sitting in the stands with Kyle and me?

Neither one of us said anything until we'd cleared the city limits and were doing fifty-five. Smooth dry hills stretched on either side of the two-lane road.

I glanced at Mom, who'd been adjusting her sunglasses about every ten seconds.

"He wouldn't like it there," I said finally. "He wouldn't be happy."

My mom reached for a Kleenex, touched it to her tongue, and, steering with her elbows, scrubbed at her Ray•Bans. "My God," she said, "who's happy?"

"I mean . . . You know what I mean. Can you see Pappy in green pants? He'd probably just die."

"I'm still considering it," she said deliberately.

"But, Mom—how can you? Everybody in town thinks he's a national treasure. Everybody but you."

She took her eyes off the road for an instant. Her glance was so intense, so focused that I looked away. "I want to keep both of you alive!" She began to pound on the steering wheel, one blow for every word. "And I don't care if you hate me and he hates me and everybody in town hates me."

I couldn't help it. My lip started to quiver. My chest heaved. My voice came out in bits and pieces. "It's not fair," I blubbered. "I was lookin' around at Alicia's party—at the other dads, I mean. And they're all so young. Kyle's dad and Walter's and Nigel's—they're not even forty. And Pappy's the only dad I ever had, and he's twice that!" I pawed at my eyes. "And if that isn't enough, he's the nicest of all of 'em." I pounded the seat with my fists. "It's not fair!"

Mom let the car slow down to maybe thirty-five. There was nobody else on the road. "Well, you're right about that," she said. "It's not fair, but it is the way it is."

She had a bottle of Evian water standing between us and she pushed it into my hands until I drank some. Mom's right hand drifted off the wheel and cradled my cheek.

"I'm sorry you didn't have a real dad."

I shook my head. "I don't care about that. Pappy

132

is a real dad. But thinkin' about not having him around just because he's old makes me crazy."

"Doggone it, Jesse. It isn't just because he's old. It's because he's getting dangerous. Don't make me into the wicked witch here. I don't have a black cat in the kitchen and a big wart on my nose. What I do have is two kids, an old one and a young one. And I can't boss the old one around like I can you."

"I'll take better care of him. I'll be more careful. Nothing else bad will happen. I guarantee."

"That's not your job. You're a kid. You're not supposed to have to watch my father."

I stared out the window, which was like turning the pages of an album because when I was ten and eleven Pappy and I had ridden all over. We'd camped at Ghost Lake, climbed Geronimo Peak, and stayed out, sometimes, for days at a time.

"Look out there," I said, pointing. "You could put me anywhere in those mountains, and I'd find my way home in no time because Pappy—"

"But that," Mom said firmly, "is the point. You could. He couldn't."

"How do you know that?" I demanded.

"Honey, I see him come out of the bathroom and stand there blinking like he just got off the plane in Rangoon. He gets lost in the house, for God's sake."

I took a huge breath. "I'd miss him so much if he wasn't around." I watched her frown as she tipped the bottle and drank. I waited, listening to the metal of the car ping in the heat. We drove for what seemed like a long time. Finally I blurted, "Go ahead and get it over with, whatever it is."

She half turned toward me, steering and talking at the same time. "Think about what I'm gonna say, okay? Don't decide now and don't argue."

I nodded.

"I know how much you love Pappy and always will. Nothing can take away what you two have had together. But time changes things, Jesse. It's not ten years ago; it's not even ten months ago. Pappy is different." She reached for my arm. "And so are you." Mom adjusted her sunglasses deliberately. "When you and I argue like we just did, what I hear is you thinking that Pappy's still going to teach you something new every day—something about camping or tracking or cowboying. Something about fairness or taking care of the land or standing up for what's right."

"Yeah, so?"

"Well, that's not going to happen, sweetheart. He's passed it along now—all of it. If I wanted somebody to take care of one of the horses, I'd ask you. If I wanted to camp, I'd take you. If I couldn't decide about something or somebody, you're who I'd go to. If I wanted the truth, I'd ask you."

Ouch. That hurt. "Pappy wouldn't lie," I stammered.

"Just the other day he told me how much he ad-

134

mires you—how you handle yourself, how you re-
spect nature, how you take school seriously, just
everything about you. He admires *you*, honey. So if
you're waiting for the torch to be passed on, stop
waiting. You've already got it in your hot little
hand."

He admires me? I sat back on the scalding vinyl
upholstery, and neither of us said anything for a long
minute.

"You and Pappy talk?" I asked finally. " 'Cause I
never see—"

"Pappy and I talk a lot. You don't see it because
you're at school or out with your buddies." Then
Mom sighed and rubbed her temples briskly. She
glanced in the rearview mirror and muttered, "I look
old-fashioned, don't I?"

"I don't think so."

Checking the deserted road, she leaned in again
and let one hand bounce off her hair, like somebody
testing Tupperware. "That's old-fashioned." Then
she rubbed two stiff, strawberry-colored strands between her fingers. "I've just about forgotten what
color this really is."

"Brown."

"You're kidding."

"I remember your old hair. I liked it."

"My *old* hair?"

"Okay, your previous hair."

All of a sudden Mom eased off the asphalt onto

the smooth dirt shoulder, then stopped under a stand of trees that hadn't seen rain in months and months but still survived and grew. "Come here, please."

I knew what was coming. "Are you hugging me or am I hugging you?"

"We're hugging each other, smart guy."

I looked around to make sure nobody from the school paper could see this. But the coast was clear, so I slid over and put my face in the crease of her neck. I mumbled into her blouse, "What you said earlier about me and everybody hating you? Nobody hates you. Don't think that."

"Good. Thank you." She kissed me on the forehead. Hard. "You know, what turned me off most about Golden Shadows was when you told Mrs. Mellon that Pappy liked Dorothy Hamill's behind and she flinched. I thought, Grow up, lady. He might be old, but he's not dead."

"So you're not puttin' him there?"

Mom sighed. "It's a lot of money, which you could use for college. And something at Golden Oaks will open up by Christmas; so, until then, maybe we should just look for a sale on fire extinguishers."

It was my turn to finally smile.

A few days later, I leaned into my mom's car as it idled in the driveway.

"I still don't like this," she said.

"Nothing's gonna happen. I'll keep an eye on him." I patted her on the shoulder. "You've been talkin' about this seminar forever."

"Yeah, but we've just had a fire and my father won't get out of his bed."

"Exactly. So watchin' Pappy now is like watchin' television. There's no reason for you to stay home."

She looked at me. "You sound funny. Are you okay?"

I rubbed at my nose. "I never saw Pappy give up before, not ever."

Mom nodded thoughtfully. "When I'm getting ready for bed and I glance down at my legs sometimes, I can see these little blue spider veins, and I know I'm getting older." She raised her brown eyes. "Now, what I do is buy another color of panty hose or I have my hair done different—any little old thing so I don't have to think about it." She took a deep breath. "But Pappy sees worse than spider veins, honey. In a way, he's lucky to be as together as he is at eighty-two. In another way, he's not so lucky because he's a witness to his own decline—you understand? He sees himself slipping, and there's nothin' he can do." One of her hands slid over mine. "You've read enough books to know that not everybody's story has a happy ending."

I looked over the roof of the car. Above the setting sun, boxy-looking clouds were stacked like paragraphs on some huge computer screen. "I guess I know it. I just don't like it."

Mom straightened up and put the gearshift lever into drive. She crooked a finger, and I leaned toward the car. She grabbed me by the neck. "You're a blessing to me, Jesse." Then she kissed me on the ear so hard that I thought I'd just about gone deaf.

I watched the taillights disappear, shook my head till the ringing stopped, then strolled indoors. Passing Pappy's room, I hesitated, then leaned close. For the first time in days, I could hear him moving around.

Carefully, I peeked in. Everything looked the same—the gun rack on the east wall, an old wood-burning stove from the Bouquet Canyon house, two stiff lariats looped over the half-open closet door, a worn braided rug with a permanent shadow where a dog named Rio used to sleep, an empty coal-oil lamp, a rocker, and a scarred chest of drawers.

But Pappy was out of bed, dressed in a pressed white shirt and jeans. He stood in front of the mirror and brushed at his hair two-handed, using palm-sized, silver-backed brushes, each one with a big *O* on the back. *O* stood for Otis, his first name, which had gotten old with him and, like he had in a way, gone out of style.

I knocked once and stepped in. "Are you going somewhere?" I asked.

He nodded. "Downtown to play cards at the Long Branch."

"I thought you were depressed. You told me you never wanted to get out of bed again."

Pappy turned to face me. He'd lost some weight, and little shadows gathered in the hollows of his cheeks. "I was about as low as a snake's behind. But I got tired of it. Got tired of myself. And between you and me, all I was doin' lying there like a summer squash was showin' your mom she was right and I should be carted off to some home." Then he started for the door.

"Put your boots on!" I said, going to fetch them for him, setting them right in front of him, letting him lean on me like he always did, while I said,

"We're supposed to stick together. I told Mom we would. But I can't go into the Long Branch."

Pappy licked his lips, then toyed with his mustache. "How long's your mom going to be at that aquapressure seminary?"

I corrected him. "Acupressure seminar. Till Sunday night."

Pappy winked. "Fine. I'll be back by then."

"But what if something happens? What if you feel weird or . . ."

"Somebody'll carry me home," he said reasonably. "Half the town knows I'm not quite what I used to be, and the other half knows, too, but they forgot." Then he grinned. "And if the Long Branch goes up in smoke, the fire department's just down the street."

He slipped through the door and, before I caught up, he was in the living room, standing and looking around.

I warned him. "If you say, 'What happened here?' I'm gonna tie you to the refrigerator."

"I know what happened. I was just figurin' how much I had to win to fix things up again. You think a thousand would do it?"

I couldn't believe it. "A thousand dollars? Pappy, you've been playin' poker for years and you've never won a thousand dollars."

He glanced at me sideways. "I never told you I

won a thousand dollars. That's different from never winnin' it."

"You honest-to-God won that much?"

Pappy fastened his long hair back with his Zuni clip. "Maybe."

"What happened? Did you lose it back?"

"Maybe I got some of it in an envelope with *Tuition* written on the outside."

I followed him toward the kitchen door. "My tuition?"

"Well, be more fair to divide it up among all my grandchildren."

"*I'm* your only grandchild."

"Oh, well. Then I guess it's all yours." He patted me firmly. "Don't wait up, now."

I yelled after him, "For an old guy who's supposed to be losing it, you're pretty cunning."

He didn't even bother to turn around; he just raised one hand as he headed for the corral. "Thanks. I feel pretty cunning tonight."

I hustled back inside and dialed Kyle's number. "Pappy just split," I explained. "Wanna help me keep an eye on him?"

"Did Elvis want a cheeseburger?"

"Meet you in five minutes."

I changed into a clean shirt, then rode my bike as fast as I could over to Kyle's. He was waiting for me under the big olive tree outside his house.

"I thought your mom said Pappy was clinically depressed," he said, cruising up beside me.

"Well, he just got clinically undepressed."

"Did he wander off tonight, or . . . ?"

I shook my head hard. "He seems fine. Said he was gonna play cards down at the Long Branch. But . . ."

"Cards? Oh, my God, I can hear it now: 'Who opened?' 'Who's Jack, and why is he better?' 'Is that a flush, or is it just hot in here?' He hasn't got the deed to the house with him, has he?"

"Just my college money."

Side by side, we shot across Norbu—down H Street and past a really cheap motel; past the Dairy Queen with a carful of high school kids parked in the gravel lot; past the tiny library, which was only open two days a week; and past the decrepit movie theater, until we could see the Long Branch Saloon with its huge plywood steer horns and phony Western front. I stopped under the awning of Red Wing Shoes, which had closed up right after Christmas and stayed closed.

I pointed. "There's Cody."

"Okay," Kyle said. "Here's the plan: we get inside somehow, go right to the table, and while you ask how to spell *Alzheimer's*, I grab Pappy's teeth and the IOU for Cody, and we get him out of there."

"Let's hope it's not that bad."

I checked the doors of the saloon. Somehow they

looked bigger than I remembered. A few couples passed us, and two girls in short skirts and white boots hurried by, laughing. We watched them stop, read the big hand-lettered sign that said FIGHTS TO-NIGHT—CASH PRIZES, then look at each other, wet their lips simultaneously, and push through the swinging doors.

"We're not even thirty if you add us together," Kyle pointed out.

"We gotta try."

A bloodthirsty roar from the Long Branch made us glance that way, then back at each other. Kyle grabbed my T-shirt and tugged. "C'mon. The worst they can do is throw us out."

We made our way past an out-of-business sporting goods store. In the window two dusty mannequins stared down at a fire made out of red cellophane. Then I pushed open the swinging doors. They'd been white, before ten thousand hands had shoved them.

Inside, we stopped and looked around, wrinkling our noses.

"Man," I said, "what's that smell?"

"Beer spilled during the Pleistocene era."

A bartender in a tank top glanced our way as we took in the two pool tables and an old pinball machine with a tiger on the back glass above the words *Jungle Fury*. There were maybe a dozen tables, with the chairs pushed every which way. A few drinks stood by themselves beside empty cigarette packs held fast to the tables by Zippo lighters. The place looked like it had been evacuated.

"What do you kids want?" shouted the bartender as, out back, the crowd shrieked.

"Lookin' for my granddad," I replied.

"You can't miss him," Kyle said. "He's playin' cards and he's probably down to nothin' but his boots by now."

"I've, uh, got his medicine."

The bartender slumped like he was about to make a decision that would haunt him for years. "Well, get it over with."

We hurried through the long dim room, which was lit mostly by beer signs featuring waterfalls. A double door big enough to back a truck through led us outside, where nearly a hundred people, most of them men, were staring up at a makeshift boxing ring. Strung around the outside of the place were tired-looking Chinese lanterns.

Kyle nudged me, and we made our way toward the other side, keeping close to the cinder-block wall, which had once been painted with dancing senoritas and dashing vaqueros, now nearly faded away.

Just then the bell rang and Walter's father—in paint-splattered cutoffs and tennis shoes with no socks—stalked toward a Hispanic guy in nothing but his jeans: no shirt, no shoes, no socks. The crowd hooted and shouted. Some people held up money

144

for side bets as the fighters were introduced: Leon and Jacinto.

The two boxers circled each other, throwing light little open-handed punches. Then Leon lunged, stood on his opponent's foot, and began to really pound him. Blood erupted from the corner of one eye. Howling, Jacinto's friends threw themselves on the edge of the canvas, but were pulled back. A beer bottle rolled toward the fighters as Leon shrugged his woozy opponent free, then hit him one last time as he fell.

As the bell clanged—I could see someone pounding it with a little hammer—a man wearing a long-sleeved white shirt climbed into the ring, held up one hand, and crowed, "Another knockout for Norbu's great white hope."

He waited as the crowd applauded and booed. "One hundred dollars," he announced, taking a bill out of his shirt pocket, "to the man who can stay three rounds with Leon." He took a quick look at his watch. "And now let's take a little pause for the cause while you he-men think it over. Cold beer inside, folks." Then he climbed out, kicking wadded-up potato-chip bags as he did.

Kyle nudged me. "There's Pappy."

In the far corner sat a felt-covered table. Even littered with poker chips, it was still the cleanest, neatest thing in the whole place. My granddad had his back to us. Besides him, there were Bobby Yates and two guys with the same straight black hair and pointy noses. But one was fat, the other thin. They were like the Before and After pictures. Both of them wore khaki shirts soaked through like they'd been trekking in the Amazon.

Pappy tossed a handful of chips on the pile, then fanned his cards on the table. Everybody else flinched like they'd gotten simultaneous penicillin shots and slammed their hands down. Pappy raked in a handful of chips and proceeded to stack them beside the others.

"Another deal or two like that," Kyle said, "and you're in Harvard."

"You think he won all those?"

"They sure didn't give 'em to him just to be nice."

"So what do we do now?"

Before Kyle could answer, I heard my name from halfway across the room. "Jesse!"

Walter climbed down out of the ring, threw a sponge into a water bucket, and led Paul toward us.

"What are you guys doin' in here?" I asked.

"Workin' my dad's corner," Walter said. He was wearing a huge shirt, with only the top button fastened. It opened like a tent flap onto his pale chest and baggy shorts. "I heard," he said, "that Pappy set the house on fire."

"Me, too," Paul said. "Did he really burn the whole thing down? Are you guys living in tents, or what?"

146

"Give me a break. It was just this little accident. Could've happened to anybody. The fire department had it out in about a minute."

"So is your granddad okay?"

"Are you kidding? Check out that pile of chips in front of him. If Mom could see him now, she'd never rag on him again."

"Pappy should run away," said Walter, "and live with wolves. That way nobody'd bother him anymore."

"Good idea, Walter," said Kyle. "Maybe he should take his candy pajamas, too."

Walter's face scrunched up. "Well, then he should be a sailor or something."

Half a dozen people edged past us. "Eighty-two," I pointed out, "isn't the best age to enlist in the navy."

"I meant like in *The Old Man and the Sea*. That Santiago guy was old, but no way did he belong in a home. I'll bet Pappy'd rather die doing stuff he really likes."

"He's not dying!"

"I didn't mean die like in *die*," Walter explained. "I meant die like in . . ."

"Decline," said Kyle.

"Yeah, right. He was pretty cool when we all went up by Colton. So I meant like instead of, you know, just declining, he should do stuff like we did that day. Outdoors and all."

"Which brings us back to living with wolves?" asked Kyle.

When we heard the sharp clang of a bell, Walter grabbed Paul and they hustled back toward the ring.

The crowd milled around. Laughter burst out here and there like little brushfires. Kyle eyed some black guys sitting together on what used to be an outdoor barbecue. Each held his money folded tight over one finger.

"Your mom," I observed, "wouldn't like the way this place is integrated."

"We should get *your* mom in here. She'd dance everybody into equality."

I could hear and partly understand half a dozen Hispanics trying to convince a big, soft-looking guy to get into the ring and knock Leon out.

Just then the bell clanged again, and the referee motioned to Leon and an oil worker with a big red beard and a beer gut.

"The great white hope takes on the great white dope," Kyle suggested as Walter's dad threw the first punch.

I heard the gloves land with a squishy sound that made me wince. I watched Leon duck a roundhouse right by the bearded guy, then step inside and hit him twice. Down he went, and his head bounced off the dirty canvas. The crowd groaned, and twenty seconds later just about every beer bottle in the place registered empty.

Just then somebody swore so loud that a dozen heads turned to see who it was.

"Damn it, Pappy!" yelled Bobby Yates, standing up with his hands balanced on his hips.

Kyle and I slipped through the crowd until we were close enough to hear everything. And see everything, too—like the even bigger stalagmites of chips in front of Pappy, and the empty place in front of Bobby, flat and green like an old grave.

"Who dealt that mess?" Bobby asked nobody in particular. Then he turned to my grandfather. "You didn't used to play this good."

"Got real old and forgot all the rules. Playin' by intuition now."

The thin man in khaki adjusted his sunglasses. "Pay up and let's get outta here. I've had enough local color to last me a lifetime."

While the two men that Kyle and I had never seen before took out some money and dropped it in front of Pappy, Bobby drained his thick-bottomed glass and patted his pockets.

"You'll have to take an IOU, Pappy."

Pappy stood up and folded a big wad of cash into his jeans. "Fine with me."

Bobby wiped his red, loose-looking lips with the back of his hand, then scrawled something on a napkin and handed it to my grandfather. "I'd appreciate it if this was between you and me, not you and me and Dad. Just come on by sometime, and I'll take care of everything."

Pappy straightened the crumpled paper. "Whatever you say."

On the way out, Bobby drained one of the drinks the others had left. Then he pushed through the crowd, shaking his head and muttering, "I'm gonna have to give this up if I can't beat some old coot who can't remember three of a kind beats two pairs."

Pappy turned around and saw Kyle and me standing there. "Hello, *compadres*," he said. "How am I doin'? You boys want a Coke or something?"

"Sure. How much did you win?"

"Just about what I needed," he said, "counting this here piece of paper." He patted one top pocket, then the other, then the first one again. "I quit smoking," he said to me, only half kidding. "So what am I lookin' for?"

"Bobby's IOU. It's in your pants pocket," Kyle said. "The right front."

"Does Bobby ever win?" I asked.

Pappy shrugged. "Everybody wins sometime, but he makes dumb bets." Then he shrugged. "Well, Bobby hasn't had an easy go of it."

As Pappy started toward the bar, Kyle said, "Hasn't had it easy? Are you kidding, Pappy? His dad used to be the richest guy in town. Bobby got a Corvette for just graduating high school."

Pappy put his arm around Kyle's shoulders as we all headed out. "Lot of strings attached to that little car, too. Had *Be like me* written all over it in his daddy's hand. Bobby's not a bad man, but he's gettin' desperate. Been that way, I think, for a while now. Drivin' him to drink and God knows what all."

We were halfway through the big, empty room when I said, "Speaking of drinks, you were gonna buy us Cokes."

Pappy stopped and scratched his head. "Let's go down to that Dairy Queen." He patted his back pocket. Then he frowned. "Where'd all that money go?"

"Pappy," said Kyle, "the money's in your pants pocket and the IOU's in—"

Granddad stood by an empty table and started to empty his pockets. All of them. "That's more like it," he said, wrapping a rubber band around the folded wad of bills. Then, as he picked everything up, he knocked the IOU off the table. I retrieved it for him.

"I knew that was down there," he said.

"Sure, Pappy."

Outside he turned left. "What about Cody?" I said.

"What about him?"

I pointed to his old roan.

"Imagine that. Came down here all on his own just to meet me."

I was just about at the bottom of the sea when the phone rang, so I had to glide up through all those pretty fish. By the time I finally broke through the surface, I was gasping for air.

That's why Mom asked me if anything was wrong.

"No; I was dreaming about swimming, that's all."

"Is Pappy okay?" Her voice was so clear and sharp, she could have been standing right next to me.

I ran one hand over my sleep-crinkled face. "Sure."

"Let me talk to him."

I looked down the empty hall with its boot-scarred floor. The door to Pappy's room was open and I could see his bed, made up neatly.

"Well, he's, uh, in the shower."

"Good. At least he can't set the soap on fire."

"Yeah, right. So, listen—how are you?"

While she talked, I hustled over to the window in my bare feet. The new carpet, probably indoor-outdoor asbestos, was rough. A few yards away, the world baked as usual. Marky Mark stood by himself under the ramada. Oh, man. Now where did Pappy go?

I held the phone to my chest for a second, and when I took it away, it made a wet sucking sound, like a tentacle.

"What was that?" Mom asked. "Are you sure everything's okay? I just keep thinking I shouldn't have come here."

I switched the phone to my other, drier hand. "But you should've. You never get away. All you do is work. Are you having a good time?"

She waited before she answered, "It's fine. But my hair looks funny."

"Did you get to acupress any cute guys?"

I heard her sigh. "Is he out of the bathroom yet?"

"Uh, no." I was sweating, and not just from the heat, either. Lying was hard work. I took a deep breath. "How's your hotel? Is it nice? Are you learning cool stuff?"

"It's all right. My room has a view, and the seminars are interesting. It's just—"

"Look, try to have a good time. You're home day after tomorrow. No biggie."

"I miss you, Jesse. I miss Pappy, too. Have him call me right back."

Oh, no! "Well, sure. But, you know, he has to wash everything. And then dry off."

"So?"

"And then shave and all. Plus get dressed."

"So?"

"So it takes time. And you don't want to miss anything. And I already took a couple of messages for him." I stared down at the blank notepad. "Couple of guys want to talk about cattle."

"You sound funny."

"I've been readin' the comics with breakfast."

"I thought you said you were asleep."

"So I was dreaming about breakfast. No wonder I'm still hungry. Look, just don't worry. I won't let Pappy out of my sight. I told you I'd take care of him, and I will."

When I hung up, I was drenched. I must have lost five pounds in ten minutes. The new Liars' Weight-Loss System. Jenny Craig, look out.

Still in nothing but my boxers, I prowled the house and then my mom's apartment. No notes anywhere. No Post-Its on any door. He was gone.

Ten minutes later, I slid off Marky before he'd even come to a stop and ran toward Kyle, who was waiting on his back porch.

"You've got your T-shirt on backward," he said.

"And Mom is gonna put my head on backward if we can't find Pappy."

Kyle scratched his head. "Are you sure he's not just in the bathroom? My dad goes in there with a magazine and—"

"No way. Cody's gone, and his everyday boots are gone."

154

"Well, I called the Long Branch, like you said."
He shook his head. "Nobody's seen him since last night."

"He's not lost."

Kyle cocked one eyebrow. "Really. You don't know where he is, but he's not lost."

I nodded. "Even when Pappy has these, you know, little spells and all, he's still locked on to something. He's not like a dog just runnin' all over the place. So wherever he is, he's goin' someplace."

"Like down to the store that's not there anymore to pick up those pants he put on layaway thirty years ago?"

"Sort of, smart guy. Except that it's almost never in town."

"So he's headed for the Santa Rios?"

I held out a clenched fist, and Kyle tapped it with his. "Exactly! And he always goes up G Street until it runs out. We can pick up his tracks there."

Kyle walked toward the barn and Surfer Boy. "And if we can't?" he asked over one shoulder.

"Don't even think that. I've got to get him back in time to call Mom."

When G Street ended, we skirted a few acres of irrigated pasture and headed for the beige-colored foothills. I could tell a Jeep Cherokee's tire prints from some old pickup's, but there was still too much of that kind of traffic for any other kind of tracking. It'd get better when the road faded away completely. Or I sure hoped it would.

But we hadn't ridden very far when Kyle reined up hard. "Look at that!" he said, pointing to a big flat place in the dust. "Heather's been here in her new shoes."

"We're looking for Cody shoes, bro, not Heather shoes."

Another ten minutes and I had just started to imagine what it'd be like to try and explain all this to Mom when I yelled, "This is him!"

Kyle frowned down. "Which ones?"

"Look! Cody's got a real long stride and he toes-in a little on his back left. Pappy stopped here and took a drink out of his canteen or something."

"That's not from last week or last year?"

"No. Too crisp. See how all the other ones are kind of blurry-looking around the edges? Cody made these this morning." I squinted into the sun.

"You look like you're about to spot the Comanches who are tryin' to stop us from taking the gold to the white-eyes who want to shoot all the buffalo."

"Will you just come on."

We rode slow so that I could sort out the right tracks from the wrong ones. Once when I got off Marky to take a real close look, Kyle said, "Weird, isn't it? Pappy teaches you all this stuff, and then you end up usin' it to find him."

As we moved on, I thought about what Kyle'd said and what Mr. Wright would've called the irony of it all. Then I started thinking about other stuff—Pappy and Mom. And me. I slowed down a little and let Kyle catch up.

"Look," I said, "I find him, take him home, he'll call Mom, and that's that. No more lying."

Kyle grinned over at me. "Cool." All of a sudden he slowed down and shielded his eyes. "What's that?" he asked, pointing.

So much heat was coming off the ground in shimmery waves that the air looked like Saran Wrap, but I could see this faint, kind of tentative line in the sky.

"Where there's smoke, there's Pappy," I said, and we headed that way.

Sure enough. There was the tripod of stones he always made for the coffeepot. I stepped off Marky, hunkered down, felt the scorched earth, then grinned up, relieved. "He left here about ten minutes ago."

Kyle scanned the dirt, then pointed. "And he went thataway."

"He's goin' to Bobby's!" I exclaimed.

"Sure. To collect from last night."

I slid into the saddle, we both shook our reins at the horses, and we coverd a mile in just under ten minutes. But when I finally spotted Pappy on the road to the Yateses' place, I pulled Marky Mark right up.

Surprised, Kyle looked over his shoulder, then made a big looping circle, and stopped beside me. "I thought we wanted to find him." He pointed. "Well, there he is."

"I was just thinking—maybe it's better if we sort of bump into him right about here."

Kyle looked around, then wiped his forehead. "Bump into him? This isn't exactly the bustling hub of corporate America."

I squirmed a little. "Well, that way I could tell Mom how he won the money on his own and collected it on his own and is gonna buy a new couch with it on his own. It makes him look, you know, competent."

"Jesse, he wasn't supposed to be winning money. He wasn't even supposed to be out of the house." He squinted at me. "I thought you weren't going to lie anymore."

"I think I said, 'We find him, we take him home, and that's that.' Well, we're not home yet."

"So you're getting a lifetime's worth of lying done in these last waning moments?" He held up one hand. "Don't say anything; I don't have my polygraph kit with me." Shaking his head, he spit—or tried to. Then he turned back. "Anyway, I thought your mom was hot to have him call her. If we wait for him to collect, it's just gonna take longer."

"I can say we tried but the line was busy."

"At a hotel?"

I leaned over, grabbed his wrist, and held on tight. "Trust me on this, okay?"

He closed his eyes, took a deep breath, then—sounding totally unconvinced—said, "Okay."

Just then Pappy rode under the arch with the big flying *Y* on it, topped a little rise, then slowly disappeared, his hat last, like somebody calmly drowning. We oozed that way ourselves until we could look down at the Yateses' big white house and barn.

Pappy was just sitting on Cody right in the middle of this horseshoe-shaped driveway. Maybe ten yards away was a green Land Rover. It was parked half in a flower bed as though the driver had come in pretty drunk.

"Go up to the front door," I whispered, "get the money, and head back this way."

"C'mon, Pappy." Kyle was willing him on, too.

When he swung down off Cody, we said it together: "All right!" But we groaned together, too, as he started for the water trough, stopped, scratched his head, looked toward the barn, headed that way, stopped.

"Oh, man."

"Make up your mind, Pappy."

"Think we ought to ride down there?" Kyle asked.

"Just hang on a minute."

"Sorry, I forgot—competent. Maybe he'll paint the fence and cure cancer. That would do it."

Just then Pappy started for the house. I grinned. "Look at that, smart guy. He'll be out in no time, and then we're home free."

But he hadn't taken half a dozen steps before he stopped, whirled around, and made a beeline for the barn.

I dropped my reins in exasperation as he disappeared inside. "Now what!"

"Jesse, sittin' here like this is making me nuts!"

"All right, all right." I clucked to Marky. "So we'll bump into him in Bobby's front yard."

As we rode up, I took in the flaking paint on the barn. Wire planters that used to hold begonias hung empty like the skeletons of some peculiar round animal. We'd just slipped in beside Cody, and I'd just sneaked a good look at the house to make sure everybody was still sleeping it off, when Pappy came out of the barn at top speed. He had his hat in one hand. His hair had come loose and was flying all over the place. He looked really weird.

Kyle and I glanced at each other as he ran right up to me, clutched at my stirrup, and said, "There's a tiger in there, boys."

"Right, Pappy."

"That's why Roberto and I can't get that herd together. That there beast has run 'em all off."

"Who's Roberto?" hissed Kyle.

"Guy who's been dead for about forty years."

Kyle lifted an imaginary phone. "Hello, Golden Acres?" he said softly. "Do you make pickups?"

I tugged at my grandfather. "C'mon. Get on your horse. We'll go home, you'll call Mom, and everything'll be all right."

He ran to Kyle. "Listen now, I ain't that senile. Bobby's got a tiger in a cage, and he's in that barn."

Kyle took my grandfather's hand. "I know, Pappy. They're hard to milk, but the meat tastes like chicken. Pretty soon we're all gonna be raisin' 'em." He glanced at me and then at Cody.

That's good, I thought. He'll keep him busy and I'll sort of ease him onto his horse before he knows what's happening.

"Doggone it!" Suddenly Pappy backed away from both of us. His hands were poised like a gunslinger's. "All you got to do is take a look."

Just then Marky Mark began to roll his eyes and shy sideways. Surfer Boy reared, and Kyle grabbed a handful of his mane.

"Now what's wrong with these guys?" he asked, standing up in the stirrups to keep his balance.

Pappy jerked one thumb in the direction of the big, sagging barn.

Kyle squinted. "C'mon," he said. "It's just gonna take a minute."

I glanced over my shoulder. "Is everybody just gonna keep sleepin' while we trespass?"

We tied the nervous horses tight—Cody, too—and followed Pappy, who flung the little door open. I clamped one hand over my face and gasped. It smelled so bad that my eyes started to water.

"What's in here?" Kyle hissed.

Blinking, I whispered, "Wait a minute. I think I see something."

The big room began to develop like a photograph: the high, churchlike ceiling with hay piled across planks; shafts of sunlight like *Star Wars* laser rays; stanchions for cattle; stalls for horses; and then—inside what looked like a cage set up on the bed of a big flatbed truck—something moving back and forth, back and forth.

"Wow!" Kyle murmured.

Stunned, we stumbled back against the splintery door we'd just closed. I felt light-headed and let myself sink to the ground. I turned to my grandfather. "You were right all along. You really did see tiger tracks. Man, I wish Mom was here."

Pappy started for the cage, walking softly, holding one hand out in front of him.

"What are you doin'? Be careful!"

"Now that I get a second look, I don't think he's any wilder than I am," Pappy said softly.

Cautiously, we stepped up beside him. Or almost beside him. The tiger was huge, with a nose wider than my hand. He was marked nice—I could tell that even in the dim light; but his stripes weren't like

162

the ones in the coloring books. They were jagged-looking, and the yellow parts of his fur were dirty as an old sock. Then he reached out with one paw.

"Somebody's had him declawed," Pappy said.

"I don't want to sound like the first black Hardy boy," said Kyle, "but something is really fishy here. I think we ought to get our butts into Norbu fast."

"Kyle's right, Pappy. Let's go." I tugged at his shirt, but he looked at me like he'd just stepped off the bus in Katmandu. I motioned for Kyle, and we kind of surrounded him, one of us on each arm, and hustled him toward the door.

The sun just sliced into us once we got outside and headed for the horses. I ripped the horses' reins loose, planted Cody's in Granddad's hand, and gave him a leg up.

Then I heard a screen door slam, and somebody yelled, "Hey! What are you all doin' out here?"

It was the fat brother from the card game. He had a tall drink in one hand and a rifle in the other. "Let's go!" Kyle shouted, and he kicked Surfer Boy hard. I whistled to Marky, caught him on the run, and vaulted into the saddle just the way Pappy had taught me years ago.

But I didn't have much time to congratulate myself or to wish Heather had seen how cool I looked, because Kyle and I were escaping all by ourselves. No Pappy.

We pulled up, making the horses almost sit down

and fight the bit. When the dust settled, we could see that Pappy was off his horse, yelling at the guy on the porch and shaking his finger at him like a schoolteacher.

The fat guy, who looked like some kind of shrubbery in his stupid camouflage, tilted the barrel of his rifle a little higher every time Pappy took another step toward him.

I went cold all over. "This is my fault," I said, almost to myself, but Kyle heard and looked over at me expectantly. "If I'd just listened to . . . I mean, I just didn't want to believe . . ."

Bobby Yates came out of the house, took one look at Pappy, and started to yell. He was carrying a drink, too, but he threw his glass into the oleanders, he was so mad.

I told Kyle he'd better go get somebody. "Tell your dad. Or just call the sheriff."

We both checked it out one more time—Granddad still lecturing, Bobby yelling and waving his arms, the fat guy's gun pointing every which way as he took quick sips from his drink, his skinny brother halfway out the door.

"Are you gonna be okay?" Kyle asked.

"I hope so. Now get goin'."

When I rode back down the driveway, I took it really easy so that everybody would see me coming and nobody would be surprised. And they saw me, all right, and it didn't seem to make one bit of difference. The commotion kept on.

"I don't care about some old man," the fat guy said. "I paid to shoot a tiger and I want to shoot him."

"No shootin'!" Pappy commanded. "You spook those cattle, we'll never get 'em rounded up."

Bobby scowled as he said, "Will you shut up, Hubert! Every time you open your mouth, you make things worse."

"Stop yellin' at him." It was the skinny brother, also in camouflage overalls. Also with a tall amber drink in one hand. "Hubie's right. We paid for that tiger, and no old man's gonna screw this up." Then he pointed at me. "Or his mascot, either."

Bobby scowled at the other two men. "I live here, okay? And the deal was that nobody from town was gonna find out about this bogus hunt. You think I'm proud of myself?"

"So now they know, and who cares?" said Hubert, squinting down at his gun like it was a book he was trying to read. "The question is, are you gonna drive that tiger out here, or do I have to shoot him in the barn?"

"Bobby!" I said.

He didn't even look up at me. "What?"

"I just want to take Pappy home. I don't know what's goin' on and I don't want to know."

"So who's stoppin' you?" asked Hubert, waving the rifle around. "Unless you want to see me get my picture taken with an honest-to-God trophy animal."

I glanced at Bobby, who looked away. Then I said, "C'mon, Pappy."

"Yeah, c'mon, Pappy." Hubert clattered down the stairs, losing his balance in his slick loafers. When the rifle went flying, I flinched, closed my eyes, and turned away, like that was going to deflect a bullet. But the gun just landed on the grass, and Hubert ended up flat on his back, his drink held up like he was making a toast. He hadn't spilled a drop.

This tickled his brother, who staggered down the stairs, laughing, and fetched his gun for him.

"Pappy?" I slid off my horse and hurried over to him. "We gotta get out of here. C'mon."

He shook his head. "Not goin' anywhere without my cattle."

"There aren't any cattle! You're thinkin' about a whole other time. Now, please, just get on your horse."

But he pulled away from me like some kid in the mall who wanted his own way. I pulled harder; he dug in his heels.

"You all are something," Hubert said, wiping his big face with his sleeve. First he pointed at Bobby. "A rancher who can't ranch, an old fart that's at least two bales short of a load, and some little wuss to look after him."

I glared at him. "Don't call my granddad names, you fat slob."

"Hey, now." And he pointed the rifle at me, swaying a little the whole time.

Bobby stepped between us, pushing the barrel of the gun down and away from me. "Will you cut it out!"

"Get me my tiger and I will!" Hubert was so loud he scared the horses.

I got a better grip on Pappy's arm. "We're leavin', Bobby."

He fiddled with his white hat and sighed. "Why'd Pappy have to pick today to stumble in here?"

"C'mon, Granddad."

"No!" This time he plopped down on the ground and wrapped both arms around his knees. "I ain't never left my herd and I'm not startin' now."

"I want my tiger!" shouted Hubert, and he pointed the gun at the sky and squeezed off one round.

Pappy looked startled.

"Don't do that!" Bobby yelled.

"He can do what he wants," said the skinny brother. "He paid and he can do what he wants."

"Rustlers!" Pappy shouted, pointing up at the brothers.

"Pappy," I pleaded, tugging at him. "Get up."

"I want my tiger." Bam! Off went another round.

That was when, right in the middle of everything, I heard a rhythmic *thud, thud, thud.* I whirled around.

"Oh, God," said Bobby as the ostrich—head down, neck out, wings flared—bore down on him. Hubert, both eyes closed like a sissy, got the rifle up to his shoulder and pulled the trigger. Big John kept coming. Hubert was aiming wildly, squeezing off one round after another.

That's when Pappy came up off the ground, grabbed the barrel, and tried to pull the gun away. Hubert swore, pushed hard, and Pappy fell.

It was just like people say when something terrible happens—everything slowed down: Pappy flung backward in the air, the look of horror on Bobby's wide face, the glint of Pappy's silver belt buckle, the slow explosion of dust when he hit, the sickening thud of his head on the sharp edge of the bottom step.

The sound of water woke me up. Immediately I knew I wasn't home and I knew I was uncomfortable. When I squirmed on the plastic couch, Dorothy, one of the nurses at the Norbu Clinic, sat down beside me.

"Here," she said in a soft hospital voice, and she handed me a little paper drinking cup.

"Is Pappy still okay?" I asked, sitting up and peeling away a page of *Newsweek* that wanted to stick to my cheek.

"He's got the mildest kind of concussion. There's not a thing in the world to worry about. He'll be busting broncs in two weeks."

"Let's hope so." I crumpled the paper cup. "Where's Mom?"

Dorothy patted me professionally as she stood up.

"Asleep in there the last time I looked." Then she hurried toward a ringing phone as I slumped back onto the cool but sticky cushions of the sagging orange couch.

A few yards away was a bulletin board that had three things tacked to it: one was about AIDS, another about hoof-and-mouth disease, and the third advertised a dance for Parents without Partners. That was my mom and me—a parent without a partner, *and* a kid without good sense.

I tipped my head back against the cracked plastic and tried to sleep some more. A few minutes later I felt the heat pour in as the front doors opened, and almost immediately I knew that I was surrounded. When I opened one eye, my friends were standing all around me, staring down as solemnly as if they were in a funeral home.

"The greatest adventure of my life," pouted Walter, "and I missed it."

Kyle asked, "How's Pappy?"

"Pretty good, I think."

"I knew there was a tiger out there all along," Walter muttered. "But what does Kyle do? He calls his dad, who calls the police. Can his dad talk to a tiger? Can the police? No, only I can talk to a tiger. But does he call me?"

Paul put his hand on top of Walter's head, pushed down, and Walter stopped talking. "Can we see him?"

I was glad to take hold of Paul's big hand and let him pull me to my feet. "Pretty soon. Mom's still back there."

"Is she mad?" asked Kyle.

I looked down at my boots, still with Bobby Yates's dust on them. "Probably."

"I'm gonna go check out the snack machine," said Paul.

Walter hit him on the arm. "You don't eat snacks anymore."

"A cat can look at a cupcake," Nigel offered, as my mother trudged down the hall toward us.

She seemed pretty tired. Her new seminar T-shirt (PRESS HERE FOR HEALTH) sagged.

She leaned toward Kyle, put one hand to his face, and gave him a kiss on the cheek. "Hi, sweetie. Are you okay?"

"Sure."

"What's Alicia say about all this? You're kind of a hero. By the time Bobby dialed nine-one-one, you already had a car on the way."

"She says I still have to live with white folks for two weeks."

Mom laughed soundlessly and shook her head. "That's cold." Then she looked at the others. "Why don't you boys tiptoe in and see Pappy. I want a few minutes with Jesse."

When the door closed behind them and we were alone, she asked, "Are you ready to talk about this?"

"I was ready last night. You're the one who banished me to that orange Naugahyde trough."

"So, talk."

I looked at the floor. "A lot of this is my fault."

"All of it," she snapped, "if you ask me." Then she caught herself. "I take that back. I guess I'm still mad." She rubbed my arm encouragingly. "Go on."

I took a big breath, like somebody about to dive. But not for treasure. Then I blurted, "I lied a lot, and if I hadn't lied, probably none of this would've happened."

Mom nodded.

"I lied about the beans that morning you got the cheese from Mr. Simpson, remember? Pappy had burned them, and maybe if I hadn't lied then, he would've been more careful later."

"Go on."

"Well, I kept stuff from you, too. Like why we went up to the Santa Rios two days in a row. It was because I didn't want you to know he was talking about a tiger, 'cause it made him sound senile. Plus I didn't tell you how he wandered off from Kyle and me and got lost.

"And then yesterday on the phone I lied about him being around. He wasn't around; he was gone, and Kyle and I had to look for him again."

Mom rubbed her face, then her new short hair. "And you found him at Bobby's."

"Pretty much. He was trying to collect some

money he won playing cards at the Long Branch. Which I also didn't tell you about."

She let both hands fall to her sides. "My God, Jesse."

"I know I should have listened to you all along. I mean, I can stand here and say I did it for Pappy, that I wanted to keep him in Norbu and not at some awful old home. But it wasn't just for him. It was for me, too." I took one of those breaths that buckled in the middle. "And look what happened. Believe me, if I could take any of it back, I would."

My mother turned in a tight little circle a couple of times, shook her hands like they were wet, then with one thumb closed off a nostril and took two or three deep breaths before she switched sides and did it again.

Then she pulled me toward her. She wrapped both arms around me and balanced her chin on my head. She didn't say anything for a few seconds, so we just stood like that. My mother was strong, and she was holding me tight. *Really* tight.

"Are you glad everything's okay," I gasped, "or is this punishment?"

"Probably both."

Just then the door to room 139 opened and Mr. Reinhartsen, who used to be a custodian at my grade school, stepped out. He had one of those mobile IV things and it was giving him a hard time.

I slipped out of my mother's hug and held the

door for him until he could get squared away. Mom and I watched him shuffle toward the glassed-in sunroom.

"Lots of kids your age," she said quietly, "want nothing to do with old people."

"Not Kyle," I said. "Not even the other guys in our study group."

She straightened my T-shirt. "You keep trying, and you're going to turn into a nice boy."

I looked down at the tiles that were polished so bright that I could almost see my deceitful eyes. "For a nice boy, I lied an awful lot."

"I said you had to keep trying."

I looked right into her brown eyes. "I won't do it again. Honest. Not about Pappy or anything else."

She held up both hands like someone feeling for rain. "So that's that. Case closed."

I looked at the number on Granddad's room. "What do we do now?"

She nodded at the pronoun. "*We* do our best by him. He took care of me. He helped me take care of you. So it's our turn to help him." She pointed an index finger at me. "Neither one of us ever had it right about Pappy. So now I think we just take it one day at a time."

I grinned at her. "Thanks."

"Hmm. Now go and see your grandfather before your buddies wear him out. I am gonna go home, wash what's left of my hair, and send away for a bowling shirt with my name on the pocket." Then she kissed me quick and hard as usual. God, maybe that's why my mom didn't have many boyfriends. Maybe she bruised their faces with those atomic kisses of hers.

As I headed down the hall, she added, "Oh, by the way. For a month you and Pappy and I will be able to bond like crazy, 'cause you're both grounded."

I turned around. "You're serious."

She was grinning, but she was nodding yes, yes, yes.

"I thought you said, 'That's that. Case closed.' "

"I'm not like some people I know. I lie."

As I entered Pappy's room and the door oozed shut behind me, I heard Walter exclaim, "So at least the animals are safe. They're goin' to L.A., someplace called the Wildlife Weight Station, and—"

"Waystation," Nigel said. "Wildlife *Way*station."

"—and we're all gonna go down and visit them sometime." He pointed to a word printed with Magic Marker on his grimy baseball hat. "And did you know I named the tiger before he left?"

Pappy squinted and read out loud, "Tim?"

"Tim the Tiger. Cool, huh? I just kept calling him that when the Fish and Game guys drove him right through the middle of town. And did you know that Tim got away once a little while ago and a couple of Bobby's men got him back? That's when you saw the tiger tracks. And did you know that the sheriff kicked those hunters out of town and he told Bobby to shape up or he'd put him in a little room with Big John. And . . ."

Pappy took as deep a breath as he could, then let his head fall back on the startlingly white pillow.

I said, "He's gettin' tired. Meet me in a minute out by the bikes, okay?"

All my friends stepped up to say good-bye to Pappy, either shaking his hand or patting the bed like it was a part of him.

"You're an official Savage Avenger now," Walter said, "so you can hang with us anytime you want."

"I'm obliged," said Pappy as he watched everybody file out.

Then I peered down at my grandfather, who always looked not quite finished without his hat. "How you doin'?"

He smiled up at me, shifted his weight with a grunt, and the IV bottle connected to his right arm jiggled a little. "I've felt worse." Then he reached up slowly and felt his bandaged forehead. "One of George's lady friends told him, 'Scars make the body more interesting.' I always thought that was a mighty kind thing to say."

"Yours will probably be shaped like a horseshoe." Then I looked away from his blue eyes, took off my hat, and pushed at my stubborn hair. "When I think of what could've happened to you out there, I just . . ."

"No reason to think about it, son, 'cause it didn't happen."

I put my hand on his arm. "I shouldn't have tried so hard, Granddad."

"You were just coverin' up for a stubborn old coot." Then he sort of pointed past the door with his chin. "Bonnie and I talked off and on last night. She's got a dandy attitude: says this is all for the best and that there's lots to learn for all three of us."

He used his free hand to pat the old flannel night-shirt he was wearing. "Your mother brought me this so I wouldn't have to wear one of them awful hospital things where your behind gets cold."

Pappy's hand—wrinkled, spotted, knobby, cured by the sun—covered mine. "She was awful nice to me last night and this morning."

I leaned against the bed. He hadn't smoked in days and days and he still smelled like tobacco, a deep and cured smell. "She loves you. I do, too."

My grandfather struggled to sit up a little. "You know, I told your mom that I don't want to go anywhere it's Golden. But I don't want to ruin her life, or yours neither, with some kind of half-cracked baby-sittin'."

"It won't be like that. We'll just all be a little more careful, that's all."

He took a swipe at his nose with his free hand. "I like Norbu," he said firmly. "I want to live out my days here."

"That's what we want, too."

He turned over with a long, whistling sigh. Then he said, "Now I think I'll just rest my eyes for a little bit. They must be puttin' something in this." His eyes rolled toward the IV. "You go on with your *compadres*."

"Okay," I said, "but I'll just stay here, maybe, until you . . ." My grandfather's eyes closed, and his breathing got deep and steady. ". . . nod off." I grinned to myself as I finished the sentence only I could hear.

Outside, my buddies were probably staring at a cloud no bigger than a telephone and glancing at the door of the hospital, anxious to get going even though there was nowhere in particular to go.

I thought about the animals, too, by now at their new home. It would be good for the tiger; nobody could shoot him, and he'd be taken care of. But maybe not so good for Big John, who wouldn't have hundreds of acres to patrol anymore.

I wondered if that was how it would be now for Pappy and Mom and me: both good and not so good.

I looked at Granddad for a while, sleeping with his mouth partly open, the steady breath moving the fringe of his mustache ever so slightly. Sunlight through the venetian blinds fell across him in long bars. So I crossed the room quietly and tugged on the white cord.

That's when I saw that the closet door was standing open. His denim shirt was hanging neatly by itself, but lying on the floor, half mashed by his old black boots, was his hat.

I picked it up. At first, I just rolled the brim the way I remembered, but it didn't look like I wanted. So I took my hat off, laid it on the narrow counter, and eyed it to get his just right.

Then I stepped back: that was more like it. They weren't exactly the same. And they sure weren't perfect. But they both looked pretty good, if I do say so myself.